P9-BZF-823

He went to take her trembling hands in his. "It seems as if I have been seeking something for a long time without knowing what I really sought was here all along."

He kissed her gently at first and then with a hunger to which she responded wholeheartedly. At last she drew away, saying breathlessly, "You have never kissed me like that before."

Not relinquishing his hold on her he replied, whispering in her ear, "Then it is long past the time I should have begun."

He kissed her again.

PAPERBACK EXCHANGE
640 FEDERAL RD.
BROOKFIELD, CT 06804
203-775-0710

Fawcett Crest Books
by Rachelle Edwards:

LADY
OF
QUALITY

Rachelle Edwards

FAWCETT CREST • NEW YORK

A Fawcett Crest Book
Published by Ballantine Books
Copyright © by Rachelle Edwards 1983

All rights reserved under International and Pan-American Copyright Conventions. Published in the United States by Ballantine
Books, a division of Random House, Inc., New York, and si-
multaneously in Canada by Random House of Canada Limited,
Toronto.

Library of Congress Catalog Card Number: 87-91543

ISBN 0-449-21363-3

This edition published by arrangement with Robert Hale, Ltd.

Manufactured in the United States of America

First Ballantine Books Edition: December 1987

ONE

Bramwell House was a handsome building set well back from the noisy stream of traffic constantly passing along Park Lane. The courtyard in front of the mansion was crowded with elegant and mostly escutcheoned carriages. In the first-floor salon Lady Rosamund Bramwell was holding court amongst a small gathering of young matrons, all of whom were dressed in a colourful array of fashionable clothing.

They were all old friends from their débutante days, during which they had vied for the attention of eligible and wealthy bachelors. Now each had found their partners with varying degrees of success, and all had several progeny, enabling them to devote much of their time to the more important pursuits of shopping, social visiting and, of course, gossip.

"I did so enjoy seeing Maldon fall flat on his face only five minutes after he arrived at Vauxhall," Phillida Berriman said with a gurgling laugh, glancing at that man's wife.

Lady Maldon sniffed derisively. "The fool was well and truly foxed half an hour after breakfast that day."

"When is he not?" the other woman responded.

Lady Maldon looked uncharacteristically glum. "When he is sober the children scarce recognise him." The others

1

laughed, and as she helped herself to some marchpane handed round by Lady Bramwell's black page she added, "However, it is a blessing on many an occasion, for he is totally unaware of the amount of blunt I spend on my hats."

"Only on your hats, Clara?" Lady Bramwell asked in astonishment, and then enquired, "How is little Adolphus now? Has he recovered from his chill?"

"Indeed he has, and what a relief it is to me. Sir Franklyn Desmaine attended him, and Adolphus was this morning playing with his soldiers again, but for a short while Maldon and I were truly concerned for his well-being."

"Sir Franklyn Desmaine?" Mrs. Berriman asked. " 'Tis a wonder he has survived at all."

Lady Maldon bridled. "I cannot conceive what you mean, Phillida. The Prince of Wales relies upon Sir Franklyn when he is ailing, which is often, and I am told that His Royal Highness has proclaimed that there is no physician better."

Phillida Berriman smiled wryly. "My dear, Prinny's judgement is so rarely to be trusted." Lady Maldon looked about to say more when Mrs. Berriman went on, "No doubt Prinny's mind is full of The Delicate Investigation going on into Princess Caroline's behaviour."

Lady Bramwell laughed. "An investigation into *his* behaviour would be more like."

Lady Maldon who had been listening attentively rejoined, "My dears, I have it on very good authority that the Princess's behaviour exceeds even the Prince's."

"I shouldn't be at all surprised," Phillida Berriman agreed. "However, I fear that poor Mrs. Fitz will soon find herself disowned once again."

Lady Bramwell gasped. "Oh, I cannot credit that, Phillida."

The other woman looked rather smug. "Berriman has detected a little cooling of the rapture when he has been

2

in their company of late. He has it in mind that Lady Hertford is edging poor Maria out of his fancy."

The other two ladies shook their heads, and then Lady Bramwell commented, "Where Prinny is concerned there will never be a shortage of *on-dits* to enliven our days."

"Berriman is in high snuff today. Brummell actually invited him to sit in the window of White's yesterday. He has scarce spoken of anything else since."

Lady Bramwell's eyes widened a little. "La! I trust Bramwell does not know, for he will go purple with envy. To join Brummell in the window of White's is his declared ambition."

Phillida Berriman smiled smugly once again. "If I know my husband, be certain all will know of it by now. Do you not find Town exceeding dull when there's racing at Newmarket?" she declared, taking two pieces of marchpane from the proferred dish.

"My dear," Lady Maldon replied, eyeing her mischievously, "even after the general exodus of gentlemen to Newmarket there is surely sufficient number remaining to satisfy even you."

Not at all put out, Mrs. Berriman sat up. "Scoff if you wish, dear Clara, but you may be surprised to learn that one gentleman has not joined the exodus on this occasion." The others looked at her expectantly, and she added with an air of drama which was typical of her, "Max Emberay."

The others chuckled disbelievingly. "Oh tush," Lady Bramwell declared while Lady Maldon nodded her agreement. "*Emberay* never misses Newmarket."

Phillida Berriman continued to look rather pleased with herself. "I can assure you that he has certainly missed it on this occasion. I saw him myself only this morning."

Lady Bramwell was evidently crestfallen. "How odd. I do hope nothing is amiss. Now I am put in mind of it,

Eliza is exceeding late today. She is usually one of the first to arrive.''

Mrs. Berriman stretched her arm along the back of the sofa. ''I can assure you his decision to miss Newmarket has nothing whatsoever to do with dear Eliza.''

Lady Bramwell sighed, and Clara Maldon sat forward in her chair. ''There is an *on-dit* we have not heard?''

''Can you not see there is something utterly malicious Phillida is aching to divulge to us?'' murmured the countess.

''I cannot conceive why you do not already know. I'm persuaded that you do. It is very evident to anyone with eyes in her head, and has been for quite some time.''

Their hostess looked apprehensive as Clara Maldon stamped her foot on the ground. ''Oh do tell! You are being very provoking, Phillida.''

Phillida Berriman lowered her voice. ''I have it on the best authority that Max Emberay is madly in love with Marisa Tarrazi.''

Clara Maldon gasped. ''The opera singer!''

''The same,'' Phillida Berriman replied, once again looking smug.

''How famous!'' Clara Maldon responded, her eyes aglow. ''What a handsome couple they make, to be sure.''

''Stuff and nonsense,'' Rosamund Bramwell snapped. ''I refuse to believe a word of it, and you had best mind your tongue, Phillida.''

The other two ladies turned their attention to her. Phillida Berriman's eyes narrowed. ''I can assure you there is no doubt whatsoever, Rosa. Cullington confided it to me only last evening, confirming my own suspicions, and he is, as you know, one of Emberay's closest cronies.'' Lady Bramwell looked away in disgust, and Mrs. Berriman continued by asking, ''Why are you so astonished, Rosa dear? Everyone knows Emberay to be a rake of the first order,

4

and nobody pretends, least of all Eliza, that he married her for love.''

Two spots of colour were evident on Lady Bramwell's cheeks. ''You have picked up a piece of scurrilous tattle and speak of it as if it were true, which it cannot possibly be. You are only jealous because Emberay refused to respond to your flirting at the Drummonds' the other evening. Everyone saw you making a cake of yourself.''

''Oh, I care not a fig for Emberay,'' Phillida Berriman retorted, waving her hand in the air before helping herself to more marchpane. ''I was merely being civil, and if that was mistaken I am not to blame.''

''*I* think he is very handsome,'' Clara Maldon declared.

''You are not alone in thinking so,'' Lady Bramwell assured her, glancing at Phillida Berriman. ''That is why he is constantly prey to ludicrous Banbury Tales, and may I say I have never heard one so ridiculous.''

''Poor Eliza,'' Mrs. Berriman sighed, still heedless of Lady Bramwell's scorn. ''She is a sad match for such a prominent member of the Corinthian Club, but then, of course, she had the largest portion of all.''

''You have never forgiven Eliza for becoming betrothed first,'' Clara Maldon accused. ''And if I recall correctly you set your cap at him before he ever knew Eliza.''

''How could he know Eliza? She hadn't even made her début. He meant absolutely nothing to me. Poor Emberay was desperate for a fortune after his brother died leaving all those horrendous debts, and my portion was certainly not large enough to attract his attention.''

''The Emberays are happy enough,'' Lady Bramwell snapped, getting to her feet in an agitated manner. ''More than most, in fact.''

She cast a knowing look at Mrs. Berriman, who agreed. ''Indeed. I cannot dispute the fact. Eliza has a husband, an establishment of her own, and two delightful children, and Emberay has a fortune and the freedom to pursue any petticoat he fancies. They are both content because they both have exactly what they want. I don't suppose Eliza will care a fig that her husband is acting the mooncalf over this opera singer. From all I have heard he is not alone in his passion.''

Lady Maldon giggled as Rosamund Bramwell walked across to the window and gazed out. ''Two score gentlemen to my knowledge have pursued Signora Tarrazi since her arrival. 'Tis nothing. Emberay would not be so corkbrained to do anything other than flirt with the latest sensation.''

''I cannot envisage Emberay sharing his passion with a score of other men,'' Phillida Berriman replied, biting into a sweetmeat.

''Signora Tarrazi is so beautiful,'' Lady Maldon breathed.

''Two score and more may have pursued the ravishing signora but only Emberay has succeeded in capturing her heart,'' Phillida Berriman informed them. ''She is as lost for love as he.''

''Is that really so?'' Clara Maldon asked, wide-eyed.

''Cullington assures me it is so. Emberay cannot endure being from her side. As a crony of long standing he is totally perplexed by the latest state of affairs. I'm afraid, up until now, Emberay has displayed a rather cavalier attitude to the ladies of his fancy, as many of them could testify. Eliza has never had anything to fear before.''

''Nor has she now,'' Lady Bramwell told her, a mite sharply.

''Poor Eliza,'' Clara Maldon breathed. ''I am mightily relieved that it is not Maldon who is so entranced by her.''

''Stuff and nonsense!'' Lady Bramwell snapped. ''You are speaking as if our husbands are saints. Which one of them does not pursue light-skirts?''

''I shall not dispute it,'' Mrs. Berriman agreed, ''but this is far more serious. Mark my words. You may depend upon it, my dears. There is the making of a juicy scandal here."

Lady Bramwell stared out of the window as a carriage halted in front of the house. "Here comes Eliza now. We had best discuss someone else's husband from now on."

Mrs. Berriman laughed. "My dear, Eliza must know what is afoot. She is not a fool. Indeed, I have always held the opinion that she is far more shrewd than we would credit her."

"I should hate it if Maldon were to be so *obvious*," his wife declared.

"You need harbour no fears on that score, my dear," Lady Bramwell consoled. "Maldon is usually too foxed to pursue anyone."

"For once I can only be grateful for it, although there are far worse vices than drunkenness."

"I have seen Emberay foxed on a number of occasions," Mrs. Berriman observed.

"Not as often as I have seen Berriman in his cups," Lady Bramwell retorted.

When the door opened a liveried footman ushered a rather flustered-looking Marchioness of Emberay into the salon.

"Eliza, my dear," Lady Bramwell greeted her, taking her hands and kissing her cheek lightly.

"I do apologise for my lateness," Lady Emberay replied, glancing at the others and casting them a shy smile.

"Do come in and warm yourself," the countess urged with more heartiness than she would normally employ. "It is of no matter I assure you."

Lady Emberay seated herself in a chair by the fire and surveyed the gathering. Her brown eyes were wide, her cheeks pink, something not altogether related to the sharp weather. Her dark hair was fastened into a neat style and topped by a green velvet bonnet trimmed with a modicum of brown braid. She was wearing a matching velvet pelisse

7

trimmed with ermine and presented a neat if not startling figure.

The Marchioness of Emberay was not a high-flyer. She entertained well without being a brilliant hostess, and she dressed expensively but not flamboyantly. Indeed she had been known to wear the same gown on more than one occasion. As a result of her reserved behaviour she presented no threat to other ladies of the *beau monde* and as a consequence was generally well liked by her acquaintances in polite society. Her husband, by direct contrast, was a renowned Corinthian and was admired by his peers and their ladies alike. The Emberays, it was acknowledged, were a splendid couple. Without being in the least tedious, they usually contrived to evade the kind of gossip forever being attracted by others in their circle.

"We were only just talking about you," Mrs. Berriman told the marchioness, and Lady Bramwell cast the woman a warning look.

"You must consider me exceeding rude for being so late."

"We just hoped that nothing was amiss," Lady Maldon ventured, glancing nervously at Mrs. Berriman.

Eliza Emberay smiled faintly, and Lady Bramwell added, "The children are well, I take it. Children are such a worry, I find."

"They are in fine health," the marchioness responded, her smile broadening now. "My delay was in no way due to them." As they looked at her expectantly she added, "My sister-in-law, Horatia, was a trifle unwell this morning and I deemed it proper to remain to make sure of her comfort."

"If I recall correctly," Phillida Berriman ventured, "Lady Horatia is very often indisposed."

"Indeed. Horatia has a delicate constitution and her nerves are easily overset."

"Of course we did wonder about your lateness, especially as Emberay is in Town and not at Newmarket,'' Lady Maldon ventured. ''That in itself is a trifle unusual, is it not?''

The marchioness glanced at her. ''Emberay has some unfinished business he couldn't possibly leave.''

Mrs. Berriman smiled. ''It needs must be of great import to keep him from the racing.''

''Do you intend to buy a new gown for the Markingtons' rout?'' Lady Bramwell asked quickly, in an obvious ploy to change the subject.

''I have ordered three and will decide which one to wear on the night,'' Mrs. Berriman admitted.

''That is very extravagant of you,'' Eliza pointed out. ''I shall certainly buy one, although I haven't decided on a colour as yet.''

''Whatever you decide upon will be delightful,'' Phillida Berriman assured her, getting to her feet. ''Clara, dear, I think we should be going now. I need to buy some ribbons and I would be obliged for your counsel.''

The other young woman got to her feet too, and Eliza Emberay said, looking dismayed, ''Must you go so soon?''

''We have been here some considerable time,'' Lady Maldon told her.

''I must have been exceeding late. I do hope I haven't missed any interesting tattle.''

Lady Maldon almost choked behind her gloved hand, and then she disguised it as a cough. Lady Bramwell cleared her throat before replying, ''Nothing of particular interest, dear. In fact, Phillida was only just saying how dull it is in Town.''

Phillida Berriman swept towards the door. ''Ah, but I confidently predict that situation is just about to change quite dramatically.''

When she and Lady Maldon had gone Lady Bramwell drew a deep sigh, but Eliza continued to stare after them in astonishment. "What on earth did she mean by that remark, Rosa?"

"No doubt she refers to Prinny's new passion for Lady Hertford," Lady Bramwell answered quickly. "I myself doubt the veracity of the news."

"From all I have heard Prinny is still in love with Mrs. FitzHerbert. He regards her as his wife."

"Which must be very provoking for Princess Caroline." Lady Bramwell drew a profound sigh. "Fond as I am of Phillida, she can be a trifle wearing at times."

Eliza laughed. "She is not a true friend as you are, Rosa."

Rosamund Bramwell looked at her friend frowningly. "I do trust nothing is amiss, Eliza. You do look a trifle peaked."

The other young woman laughed again, with more bewilderment than before. "No, indeed. What can there be amiss? Horatia's vapours cannot be considered so, for she is ever in a taking over something or other. How my late parents-in-law contrived to produce two children as unalike as Max and Horatia I cannot possibly fathom. Dorinda is perfectly normal too."

Rosamund Bramwell laughed too then, with a great deal of relief, and they were soon engaged in a light-hearted conversation far removed from any dangerous topic.

TWO

It was a quiet time of the day in the small Bloomsbury square. Neat houses overlooked the central garden where several elegantly clad couples strolled in the cold sunshine and a number of nursemaids took the air with their young charges.

An almost constant procession of carriages and hackneys streamed in and out of the square, and outside one house stood a smart curricle bearing an aristocratic escutcheon. A liveried tiger held the reins as he paced to and fro to keep warm, for the air was sharp. Suddenly a high-perch phaeton bearing the coat of arms of the Marquis of Emberay drove down the street at a spanking pace and then drew up behind the curricle.

A tall, dark man stepped down and thrust the reins at his own tiger at the same time as staring coldly at the other conveyance. Then he threw back his caped driving-coat and strode up to the front door to give the bell-pull one firm tug. A few moments later he was admitted to the house where he handed his high-crowned beaver and driving-coat to the lackey. The marquis was considered, by those who knew him, to be a handsome man. Taller than most, his height dwarfed the narrow hall in which he was standing. His perfectly fitting coat needed no padding, nor did his skin-tight pantaloons. His coat had been made by

Brummell's own tailor and his highly polished hessian boots by Hoby, and although he wore his clothes with an apparently careless disregard nothing was further from the truth. His dark curls were brushed into a seemingly casual style, and just at that moment his eyes were dark with suppressed anger and frustration.

"Emberay! My dear fellow!"

The marquis swung round on his heel. As his eyes alighted on the man who had come out of the drawing-room he displayed no pleasure. In fact his complexion seemed to grow even darker.

"Maldon," he responded. The other man smiled and inclined his head slightly. "This place is as busy as White's these days."

"But certainly less dull, old boy," replied the other man, who went past with a swaggering walk which angered the marquis even more.

With the departure of the Earl of Maldon, Lord Emberay went quickly into the drawing-room without a further glance in the direction of the other man. Marisa Tarrazi was standing by the window, and when he went into the room she turned to face him.

"My Lord Emberay," she murmured shyly in the attractively accented voice which had entranced so many rich and titled gentlemen in the short time she had been in London.

His demeanour altered entirely when he caught sight of her. The anger went as if by magic and his stern features relaxed into a smile which had during his four and thirty years captivated countless females.

"As always you look totally ravishing, Marisa," he told her. "I don't know how you contrive after singing into the night."

"You flatter me, my lord," she replied, lowering her eyes.

"Deservedly. Oh, most assuredly so. You are unsurpassable." He took both her hands and raised them to his lips. "Marisa, Marisa, my love," he murmured. A moment later his arms went about her and his lips caressed her cheek and her throat. "I have waited for this moment since I left you last night."

She laughed softly. "It is not so long ago, *caro*."

"It is a lifetime."

She extricated herself from his embrace and drew him down onto a sofa. "I cannot tell you how pleased I am that you have called. The day has been tedious and you divert me so well."

He looked suddenly wry. "If I had not called in I doubt if you would have been lonely, Marisa."

She waved her hand in the air in a dismissive gesture. "Oh, they mean nothing to me. Maldon is a fool."

"Do you say that of me too when I'm not here?" he asked softly.

"Oh no," she answered, looking into his eyes. "I cannot be in your company often enough."

"It does my heart good to hear you say so, Marisa. I must tell you that you sang wonderfully last night."

"Yes, I know. You told me so when you were here afterwards."

"So I tell you again."

"You must know why I sang so well."

His eyes all but devoured her. "Tell me, Marisa. I love to hear you speak. Even when you're not singing it's like hearing the song of a nightingale."

She laughed. "Such flummery, but so welcome." All at once she was serious again. "You know it is because I sing directly to you. The theatre is empty for me except for you." She reached out for a posy of flowers which had been lying on a table near by. "It was so kind of you to send these to me."

"That is only a small token of my affection for you,

Marisa. There will be more, much more in the future. I want to give you the world."

"Your company is all I desire."

He stood up, walking slowly across the room. "And I know I want to be with you as often as I can contrive. Morning, afternoon and evening, whenever it is possible."

"Poor Lady Emberay," the singer crooned, looking at him coyly.

"Oh, you need not pity my wife, Marisa."

"How can I not when I have the love of her husband?"

"Eliza is perfectly understanding. I am free to do whatever I please. It has always been so ever since we were married. She has her life and I have mine."

"How fortunate for you."

"For us both," he amended. He turned on his heel to face her again. "Marisa, I will be frank with you. The notion that coxcombs like Maldon and Nuncton have the freedom to call here at all times does not please me at all."

She shrugged slightly. "What can I do about it? I cannot be rude and turn away such important people. They are the ones who pay to hear me sing."

He sat down again, taking her hands in his. "Let me provide a house of your own, Marisa. You will be independent then and have no need to grease anyone's boots."

For a moment she seemed stunned, and then she withdrew her hands from his. He watched her anxiously for a moment or two before asking, "What do you say, Marisa? Does the notion find favour with you?"

"You make me a very tempting proposition, *caro*."

"Then you will accept," he said firmly, and when she didn't reply he went on, "I adore you and I swear you shall see me more often than my own wife."

She smiled faintly, and he kissed her hands again. "Those poor ladies with their fine houses and elegant car-

14

riages. I want none of it. I want only love. It is all I want of you.''

"It is what you shall have, my love.''

"Does no one in the *ton* marry for love?''

"Not many,'' he admitted, smiling wryly. "I am more fortunate than most, however, my wife is particularly amiable.''

"Well, I am not the kind of woman who wishes to be kept by a gentleman, however charming. I am able to sing and people are willing to pay to hear my voice. I am able to support myself in this modest way. It is enough.''

"Marisa, that is not good enough for me,'' he protested, trying to keep his considerable impatience tightly in control.

She smiled faintly. "It will have to be.''

"It pains me to share you with other people.''

"That isn't so, *caro*. I love no one else but you.'' She paused for a moment before inviting, "Let us go to my private sitting-room where no one will disturb us.''

Once more he stood up, looking angry again. "I have a dinner engagement and must go home to change.''

"You are angry with me,'' Marisa Tarrazi pouted. "Please don't be angry with me, *caro*. That is something I cannot bear.''

The anger so evident on his face melted and she went into his arms. "I can't be angry with you for more than a moment.''

She sighed with contentment as she laid her head against his shoulder. "That is a great relief.''

He looked down at her. "May I call on you tomorrow?''

"I shall be devastated if you do not. I await your return with great impatience.''

A few minutes later she stood at the window watching him drive away. When she moved away from the window she was smiling and pensive. Picking up the posy she rang for her maid who appeared a very few moments later.

"Lord Emberay did not stay for very long, signora. Is anything amiss?"

"Nothing is amiss. He will be back," Signora Tarrazi assured her and then asked, still in her pensive mood, "Do you think I would make a fine marchioness, Mimsie?"

The woman's eyes widened, "Signora? His lordship cannot have come up to scratch?"

"No, but he will."

"I thought Lord Emberay was a married man."

"They all are, but Lord Emberay is so madly in love with me he will soon be determined to divorce his wife, to whom he is not very much attached, and marry me."

The woman still looked wide-eyed at her mistress's extravagant claim. "Divorce is such a serious matter in this country, so difficult, signora. Are you quite certain—"

"I am fully aware of all the difficulties involved, Mimsie, but Lord Emberay is a man who will always get what he wants and any difficulty he encounters will only serve to make him want it even more. He is very much in love with me, and when he realises nothing short of marriage will satisfy me, he will allow nothing to stand in his way."

The singer looked very pleased with herself while Mimsie contemplated the wonder of becoming lady's maid to a marchioness.

THREE

It was several days later when, as was her habit every morning, the Marchioness of Emberay was sitting at the breakfast-table perusing the latest invitation cards to arrive at her Piccadilly home. The Emberay mansion was situated in a large piece of land separated from the road by tall railings and a pair of gates wide enough to accommodate the most handsome carriage.

When the door to the breakfast-room opened Eliza looked up hopefully. Her expression did not alter when she saw her sister-in-law and not her husband enter the room.

"Horatia, my dear, how nice to see you abroad so early in the morning."

"It is only because I could not sleep. It seemed foolish to remain abed when I can only toss and turn in pain and discomfort."

As she sat down at the table Eliza regarded her pityingly. She was wearing an outmoded kerseymere gown and lace cap, neither of which became her. Eliza herself had never been considered a beauty, but Horatia was without doubt plain and appeared even more so by comparison to her flamboyant and handsome brother. When Horatia had been a girl the family was considerably impoverished and therefore there had been no means of attracting a husband for someone with so few physical attributes. Now Horatia resorted to ill health

17

as so many in her situation, which was a well-worn escape from a world in which she no longer had a place. Eliza realised all too well how easily it could happen and always went out of her way to be kind to her sister-in-law.

"I trust it is nothing serious."

"I've had one of my headaches for days," the woman explained as she surveyed the selection of breakfast-dishes before proceeding to pile her plate with food.

"You poor dear. Have you taken any laudanum? I'm persuaded a small dose would ease your pain."

"It has little affect, I fear. Nothing helps, but I live in hope, Eliza."

"I know exactly what will set you to rights, Horatia: a ride to Bond Street. I have a number of purchases to make and you must accompany me."

"Oh no. I don't believe such an outing will be of any benefit to me. Bond Street is so busy nowadays, unlike when I was a girl. All those carriages going by seem to rattle inside my head."

"Oh very well, Horatia, if it is truly beyond you at the moment I fully understand, only 'tis a great pity. You see, not only would I enjoy your company, my dear, but of far greater import is your superior taste and knowledge. You know how greatly I value your opinion and guidance when I make my purchases."

The older woman looked immediately gratified as the footman returned with fresh coffee. "I can scarce refuse such a plea, Eliza. I feel it incumbent upon me to bear you company especially since that scapegrace husband of yours neglects you shamefully."

Eliza chuckled good-naturedly. "Horatia, he is your brother and the head of this family. You really must not be so disrespectful of him."

"I must always speak the truth. I fear he favours our scapegrace father and elder brother who between them brought our family to ruin."

18

Eliza put down her cup and looked at her sister-in-law. "Max is not like that, Horatia."

"I take leave to disagree with you, and I beg you to be vigilant that Christopher does not dissipate his life too."

The woman's comment amused Eliza. "Kit is no more than a baby."

"He is a trifle wild. You must endeavour to cure him of that trait before it is too late. I warn you in all sincerity."

"You never do Max justice. I cannot in all truth expect him to accompany me to the mercers and linen drapers, and if he did I dare say his advice and counsel would be totally useless to me."

"There is no need for sarcasm, Eliza. One might, however, expect my brother to join us for dinner on the occasional evening."

The marchioness pushed back her chair as she got to her feet. "Don't hurry, Horatia. I shall be with the children in the nursery until you are ready to leave."

It was with a great deal of relief that she left her sister-in-law in the dining-room, but then her demeanour brightened again when she saw her husband coming down the stairs towards her. He was, as always, immaculately dressed, his neckcloth perfectly folded, his coat wrinkle-free, and his boots unblemished by so much as a smear. His unfailing elegance always aroused a good deal of admiration in his more mundane wife who had never aspired to sartorial excellence.

"Good morning," she greeted him.

"Good morning to you, Eliza," he responded in a warm tone. "You are up and abroad early I see."

Her eyes twinkled with amusement. "If it was usual for you to be up at this hour, Max, you would undoubtedly see me every morning."

"Well, as we are both up and abroad on this occasion, shall you join me for breakfast?"

"That is a rare enough treat, I own," she replied with true

19

regret, "but I must see the children before I go out. Mayhap you will be home for dinner and you can impart your opinion of last night's opera performance. I was sorry to have missed it."

He looked discomforted. "Alas no. I'm afraid I have a previous engagement."

Eliza's eyes widened a little. "One of import, I trust."

"By Royal command, if that can be considered so. I am invited to Carlton House for dinner. Brummell, Alvanley and a few others will be there. It will be tedious, no doubt, but I cannot cry off."

Eliza's smile faded a little. "Of course not, but you do recall we are to dine at the Fullwood's tomorrow?"

"Indeed, and you may be certain I shall be available to escort you there."

"I shall look forward to it, but for now you may join Horatia for breakfast in my absence."

He looked so horrified she was obliged to laugh. "I thought she was perpetually indisposed."

"She is in fine health today and anxious to see you."

"I'd as lief dine with the wild animals in the zoo!"

"Oh, you must not say so, Max. For all her megrims she has a kind heart and is exceeding fond of you."

"If you say so, Eliza, but at this time of the morning I'm in no mind to suffer one of her setdowns. I believe I shall go and breakfast with Cullington."

Eliza's eyes sparkled. "Tush! You are more than a match for Horatia. Besides, you won't be obliged to suffer her company for long, for she is in a fidge to join me on our shopping expedition." She paused a moment before saying softly, "I must go now and see the children."

As she made to go past him he caught her arm and drew her back gently. He gazed down into her face. "I appreciate your kindness to my sister, Eliza. I know how tiresome she can be."

Her cheeks grew slightly pink. "You have no cause to

thank me. I am exceedingly fond of Horatia and I don't find her in the least tiresome.''

She hurried up the stairs feeling oddly discomforted by their conversation. However, when she found her son marching up and down the nursery with a wooden rifle over his shoulder she was immediately diverted.

"My goodness, Kit, you do look fearsome," Eliza exclaimed as she drew back in the doorway.

He pointed the wooden rifle towards her, saying fiercely, "I am one of His Majesty's Dragoons and you are my prisoner. Do you surrender?"

Eliza raised her hands in the air. "I have no choice. I am beaten."

"I'm a colonel in His Majesty's Dragoon Guards. You're a Frenchy prisoner."

"My goodness," Eliza murmured again. "What shall you do to me, Colonel? I am at your mercy."

"Stand in the corner and be silent, Frenchy." Eliza did so, and he added, "Boney shall soon be defeated, you know. There is no hope for you."

"If every English soldier is as brave as you, Colonel Kit, it will not take long to defeat that horrible man."

The child's face suddenly crumpled. "Oh, I do hope they wait until I am old enough to take part in the war."

"I can assure you I hope it is soon ended."

"But I want to capture Boney for myself."

Eliza eyed him wryly. "Just now your place at Eton seems a long way away. Colonel, may I put my hands down now?"

"You may sit on the straw in your cell if you wish." Obligingly Eliza crouched down, and the child asked pensively, "Papa was a soldier once, wasn't he?"

"For a while."

"How tedious life must be for him now."

"Papa does not think so, I'm quite certain."

"When I am a soldier I shall never give it up, not for anything, Mama."

"Your Papa had no choice, Kit. His brother, the late marquis—died, and Papa was obliged to come home to settle his affairs. Have you seen Lucy this morning?"

The child's face took on a look of distate. "She's still having her porridge. She takes an unconscionable time eating her food."

"That's because she is very young, Kit."

"I know," he groaned. "Lucy is too small to play exciting games like this. Girls are useless, Mama. As soon as she is old enough to play really good games, Anna will insist that she sits sewing."

His mother could not resist a smile. "Never mind, dear. I shall invite the Maldon boys along. I'm persuaded they would make excellent French prisoners. They'd surrender without a fight."

"Algy Maldon is always fighting. He says his Papa is a greater Corinthian than mine. That isn't true, is it, Mama?"

"It certainly is not," Eliza replied with gusto.

"Eliza, what on earth do you think you're about?"

Horatia Stratton was standing in the doorway, looking astonished at the sight of the marchioness huddled into the corner with her skirts hitched up to reveal a tantalising glimpse of silk stockings to all who might happen to walk past the nursery.

"Mama is a French prisoner, Aunt Horatia," Kit explained as Eliza giggled. "You can be one also if you wish. There's room in the prison."

The older woman stiffened with indignation. "Certainly not, Christopher. How unseemly it is."

Again Eliza chuckled, this time more at her sister-in-law's outrage than anything else.

"Good grief!" exclaimed the marquis, appearing at his sister's side a moment later. "What *are* you doing, Eliza?"

"I'm a Frenchy prisoner captured by Colonel Kit here."

"Tell her it's unseemly, Emberay," Horatia urged.

The marquis smiled, and then cast his sister an astonished

22

look. "Kit is getting some valuable practice in the art of soldiering, Horatia. That cannot be deemed bad."

The woman gasped with exasperation. "I might have known you would approve."

The boy ran up to his father, asking, "Papa, when I am old enough may I join your regiment?"

"I am certain they will be glad to have you," the marquis replied, patting his son on the head. "If the army had more men like you, Kit, Boney would soon be routed."

The child's cheeks glowed with pleasure, and his father added, "Make certain your prisoner cannot escape."

"Oh, for heaven's sake, Max," Eliza complained. "I don't wish to remain in this corner all day."

"If you do it won't involve me in vast amounts of expense as I fear your shopping expedition might well do."

"Eliza is most abstemious," his sister scolded, and then she glanced at him meaningfully, "unlike some other members of the family."

Apparently heedless of her blandishment, the marquis straightened up, saying, "I must take my leave of you now. Contrive to escape how you will, Eliza. Goodbye, Kit."

"Goodbye, Papa."

As he turned on his heel Eliza scrambled to her feet at last. "Oh, what a pity; he did not see Lucy."

Horatia's lips were tight with disapproval. "I don't suppose Lucy or any of us, for that matter, is like to see him again for a sennight."

"Oh, don't be so Friday-faced," Eliza chided goodnaturedly just as a young child came running in from the adjoining room. "Emberay is in high snuff these days and I can only be glad of it."

"Mama!"

Eliza's face broke into a smile of delight. "Lucy, dearest. What a pretty gown you're wearing."

She lifted the little girl into her arms and hugged her tightly. "Kiss Aunt Horatia now," Eliza ordered the child, and she

23

did so, albeit with slight reluctance. However, Horatia seemed gratified by it.

"I suppose our game is over now," Kit complained.

"We shall certainly play another time soon," his mother promised, putting Lucy down again. "Your aunt and I have some important shopping to do."

"May I go riding on my pony today?" he asked plaintively.

"You may certainly do so," Eliza promised. "You shall go this very afternoon and I will accompany you."

She kissed both children once again before handing them back to their nursery-maid.

"That child is the Earl of Aldan," Horatia pointed out when they left the nursery.

"Yes, I know," Eliza replied, casting her sister-in-law a smile.

"The point I am endeavouring to make is that he should have more dignity."

"He is only a child, Horatia dear. There is plenty of time for him to become a prosy old bore."

Horatia stiffened. "Really, Eliza, this is no time for levity. That child is in need of strict discipline. You indulge him far too much for what is good for him."

Her sister-in-law's strictures had no dampening effect upon the marchioness. She merely smiled. "Yes, Horatia, I suppose I do," she replied as she went to fetch her bonnet and pelisse.

The two ladies emerged from the mercer's emporium into the cold sunlight of Bond Street where their handsome carriage awaited them at the kerbside. A footman in scarlet and gold livery waited to usher the ladies into the carriage and to their next destination.

Eliza was feeling more than a little satisfied with her purchases, which were just what she had wanted, but at the same time she had contrived to give Horatia the notion it was she who had chosen everything.

"I am still not convinced of the virtue of buying that piece of muslin for myself," Horatia murmured as she drew on her gloves.

Eliza nodded to an acquaintance who had just alighted from a curricle before replying. "It will make a delightful gown for you, Horatia. You haven't had a new gown for an age."

The woman smiled forlornly. "My needs are so few, my dear. My health allows me to leave the house so rarely, and therefore I have no need for new gowns."

"But you are so much improved of late!"

"Do you think so?"

"Indeed I do."

"I cannot concede that I am. I have lost count of the times I have been given notice to quit."

"Ah yes, but you are still with us, Horatia, for which we must give thanks."

"That might well be so, my dear, but for how long?"

It was with some relief that Eliza caught sight of Phillida Berriman emerging from a shop farther down the street. "La! How angry Berriman will be when he receives the vouchers for this morning's work," she declared as she approached them. "However, by the time he returns from Brighton 'tis to be hoped he will feel too euphoric to care."

"Has he gone to Brighton at this time of the year?" Eliza asked, frowning perplexedly.

"Lady Hertford wished it and you know Prinny can refuse her nothing at the moment. He will doubtless also wish to take part in military manôeuvres on the Downs. You know how well he enjoys his war games. Naturally Berriman was in a fidge to go too. There will be unending gaming and drinking." She glanced slyly at Eliza before adding, "I am only surprised Emberay did not wish to join them too."

Eliza was still looking too puzzled to take any note of Mrs.

25

Berriman's irony. "I had no notion that the Prince was in Brighton."

Phillida Berriman laughed. "Have I not only just told you that he is? They all raced down two days ago. I don't suppose we shall see them in Town for a sennight. One cannot believe Brighton to be healthy at this time of the year."

"In my opinion it is unhealthy at any time of the year," Horatia told her, sniffing derisively.

Mrs. Berriman smiled sweetly. "I'm certain you must know better than anyone, Lady Horatia. La! I must leave you now, but no doubt you will be at the Fullwood's soiree tomorrow, so until then. *Au revoir.*"

She waved as she hurried away towards her barouche, leaving Eliza on the pavement, still frowning worriedly.

"That baggage!" Horatia declared. "I doubt if she will be obliged to pine alone while her husband is away."

"How odd," Eliza reflected thoughtfully. "I was so certain Max told me he was dining at Carlton House tonight."

"Unless he is dining there alone, I take leave to doubt it."

"No doubt I mistook what he told me," Eliza conceded, casting her sister-in-law a smile which was not returned.

Horatia looked characteristically tight-lipped. "I cannot conceive why Emberay has taken up with that terrible man."

Her outrage caused Eliza to look both amused and astonished. "Horatia, dear, you are talking about our future King. My husband can scarce disregard him."

"I shudder whenever I contemplate that dreadful man will one day be King. Such a rake, so dissipated, he's quite unlike his poor father who is sadly deranged."

Eliza gave her an indulgent look. "I own I am not overly fond of the Prince myself, but I do understand why Max wishes to cultivate his friendship."

They climbed into the carriage, and Horatia sank wearily into the squabs with a sigh. Sympathetically Eliza told her, "You must go directly home and rest, my dear."

"Indeed I shall. I am quite done up. It really has been the most trying day."

She drew another profound sigh, glanced out of the window and then sat up straight again. "Eliza, is that not Emberay I see over there?"

Eagerly Eliza peered from the window too, and sure enough it was her husband who had just come out of an establishment at the other side of the road. Her heartbeat quickened at the unexpected sight of him.

"Why, he must have been to Gentleman Jackson's Gymnasium," she declared, not troubling to hide her pleasure.

"Such foolishness, indulging in fisticuffs for pleasure. I cannot conceive why the way gentlemen spend their time."

"No doubt they regard our need to shop for ribbons on our bonnets or lace for our petticoats as gross foolishness too." Eliza glanced out of the window again and waved to attract his attention. However, he was looking in entirely another direction, and Eliza's smile faded somewhat at the sight of him greeting a lady who approached. His smile was unmistakably that of a man delighted to see the other person. He raised one of her hands to his lips, exchanged a few words and then with great solicitude handed her into his high-perch phaeton.

Eliza's own carriage jerked and began to move down the crowded street. As the sight of her husband faded into the distance, Lady Emberay sank back into the squabs at last, her eyes troubled by what she had witnessed, although she wasn't quite certain why.

"Who is that creature?" Horatia demanded. "Why did Emberay take her in his carriage?"

The marchioness stared at her blankly. "I don't—" Then she sat forward. "Yes, I *do* know who she is. She looked very much like Signora Tarrazi, the opera singer. I have heard her sing on several occasions of late. Yes, I am certain it was she."

Lady Horatia looked outraged. "Indeed."

27

"You saw her sing Cherubino in the Marriage of Figaro. You must recall the occasion."

"I most certainly do. The box was so shockingly draughty I contracted a chill and was confined to my bed for days afterwards."

"That was most unfortunate, but Signora Tarrazi is regarded as second only to Catalini. Indeed, there are many who rate her more highly. Of late she is quite the talk of the Town."

"That might well be so, Eliza, but it does not explain why Emberay is making so much of her."

"I expect it's because he admires her as we all do. He has often praised the power of her voice whenever we have heard her sing."

"And you say she has become all the crack?"

"Undoubtedly."

"I cannot concede that. Her voice is far too shrill for true greatness. I cannot own that she is near to Catalini."

"It is all a matter of opinion, Horatia. She cannot please everyone."

"You do realise what is happening, don't you, Eliza? Those so-called members of the Corinthian Club will be competing for her favours, and naturally Emberay is determined to win any wager involved."

Eliza stiffened. "I don't see how you can possibly know."

The older woman looked smug. "My dear, I know my brother."

Turning her face away, Eliza drew a sigh, realising too it was just the thing in which the marquis was likely to become involved, and the notion did not please her at all.

FOUR

The marquis drove his splendid carriage down Bond Street unaware that his wife and sister had seen him. He was only aware, and pleasurably so, of the curious glances he was attracting at all sides. One of the people who saw him drive by was the Countess of Bramwell who took no pleasure at all in what she saw, unlike Phillida Berriman who instructed her driver to make for the Maldon house immediately so she could impart this latest piece of gossip to her friend without delay.

"We are the object of a great deal of attention," Marisa Tarrazi pointed out, not troubling to hide her pleasure.

In her splendidly plumed bonnet and her fur-lined pelisse she knew that there were few people who would not recognise her and note at whose side she was riding. It was akin to his making a public declaration of their relationship.

"That is the intention," he replied firmly. "I am very proud to be seen with you."

"There are some gentlemen who might not wish to be seen in such a public place with me."

"If such creatures exist, they are fools." He glanced at her. "Tell me, Marisa, what happened to your husband? You rarely mention him."

She sighed. "Alas, he is dead. He died quite suddenly less

than a sennight after we were married, leaving me desolate and entirely alone. It was a wretched time.''

His eyes clouded with pain. "How you must have suffered.''

"I can scarce bear to think of it even now, but I was determined to survive, and I did. The good Lord bestowed upon me a voice which I am delighted gives pleasure to so many people.''

He glanced sideways at her again. "Just the sight of you would do that.''

"I wish to give pleasure only to my dearest Emberay,'' she replied, her voice soft and caressing.

"You have known so much unhappiness, my love, but I swear to you it is over now. I mean to ensure you are never desolate again.'' She sighed as he asked in a lighter tone, "It is a fine day for riding, so shall we drive to Richmond?''

She touched his arm lightly and her eyes sparkled. "I have a far better notion; let us drive to Bloomsbury. My maid will tell all other callers I am out.''

As he drove the phaeton into Oxford Street he smiled with pleasure. "That is an excellent suggestion.''

"Tell me what you do at that gymnasium. So many gentlemen go there.''

"I take lessons in fisticuffs with one of the greatest fighters who ever lived.''

"That must be why you have such magnificent muscles, *caro*.''

He smiled at her, and she asked, "Does your wife not concern herself where you are when you spend so much time with me?''

He chuckled. "Indeed she does not. Eliza leads a busy life of her own and is quite satisfied with our marriage.''

"How odd you English are.'' She paused before speculating, "Mayhap she has a lover too.''

At the suggestion the marquis threw back his head and

laughed heartily. "Eliza! You've no notion how amusing that is, Marisa. Eliza with a lover! How incongruous."

The singer looked miffed at his amusement. "I cannot conceive why you mock me, my lord. Your wife, whom I have seen, is very pretty."

"I have never considered her so. Of course, I own, she is not hag-faced, but pretty is not a word I would use to describe her, although I dare say she is pleasing enough." He glanced at her and said in a less strident tone, "Next to you, my dearest, all other women fade into obscurity."

Her cheeks grew faintly pink. "You must have loved her when you asked her to marry you."

He looked and sounded a mite exasperated. "This is England, Marisa, not Italy, although I dare say marriages are contracted in much the same way as here."

"I really do not understand why people marry except for love."

"It is quite simple. Eliza was heiress to a great fortune founded in the Indies, and her father was very anxious to marry her to a titled family. Eliza was born and brought up in Jamaica."

"You do not seem to be the kind of man to abide such a dreadful arrangement."

"I had little choice in the matter. My brother, the late marquis, had just been killed in a duel after running up the most horrendous debts. Marriage to an heiress was the only answer to my problems. We spent our honeymoon inspecting the plantations she inherited."

"My poor Emberay," she crooned. "How dull it must have been even for Lady Emberay."

He had been deep in thought, but as she spoke he looked up at her. "Eliza was quite agreeable, I assure you. No one forced her into marriage."

"You English have such odd ways. I have yet to grow accustomed to them."

"We have our own unwritten code of honour too. For

instance, I know a fellow who is cuckolding his best friend which I consider abominable behaviour for a true gentleman. I would never do such a thing.''

Marisa Tarrazi smiled faintly. ''If the husband discovers his wife's infidelity, will he divorce her?''

''I doubt it. Why should he indeed? Her husband has a friendship with a demi-rep of great beauty.''

She frowned. ''But as I understand it divorce is possible in England.''

''At great trouble and expense, and as a last resort,'' he replied, looking troubled, ''but it certainly is possible.''

''Yes, I thought so,'' the woman replied, drawing a sigh of pure satisfaction as the high-perch phaeton turned into the square.

The Marchioness of Emberay stared across the carriage to where her husband sat deep in thought. He looked particularly handsome in his evening-clothes, a large diamond pin fastening his neckcloth. She could not help but recall how shabby he had looked when she first met him. An acquaintance with Brummell had certainly changed his style for the better, she reflected.

''You look a trifle discomposed,'' she ventured at last when it appeared he had forgotten her presence.

''Is it so surprising?'' he responded irritably. ''M'sister's outside of enough.''

Although her own thoughts had been a mite troubled since the previous afternoon, Eliza was bound to smile. All her married life she had been obliged to act the peacemaker between them.

''Oh dear, what has she said now to put you out of countenance?''

''It is more her attitude, for her words cannot trouble me. Horatia is persuaded I am still in leading strings. I cannot conceive why I should be prey to her vinegar tongue merely for being civil to a lady in Bond Street.''

Eliza eyed him wryly. "From what I observed you were more than civil to her."

"Oh, I do pray you are not going to give me a setdown too, Eliza."

"Certainly not. You know me better than that."

His face relaxed into a smile. "I am considerably relieved and thank God you are not in the least like m'sister."

"I have been more fortunate than Horatia, Max," she pointed out, feeling suddenly melancholy.

He sighed. "I dare say, although I cannot envisage any gentleman being obliged to endure her company even if my father had been able to set aside a considerable portion." He became more cheerful then. "I did suggest to her that the country air might be beneficial to her health."

"Oh, Max, you never get anywhere with that moonshine. Horatia is impervious to it."

"You do me an injustice, my dear. I believe she is set to go in the very near future, and you should rejoice as much as I do, for having that bracket-face around is not conducive to contentment for either of us."

"You are not often at home to see her—or me, Max. In fact, I'm given to believe you didn't come home at all last night. Was—the Prince of Wales so desirous of your company?"

She watched him carefully, and his unease was as uncharacteristic as it was apparent to her. "The Prince, it seems, was in Brighton. I had no notion. He did not condescend to inform me although I dare say he had forgotten entirely his invitation. By mere chance I discovered he was not at Carlton House. I went to White's and was informed there of the Prince's departure from Town."

The marquis looked out of the window at the darkened street and the running footmen with their lighted torches alongside the carriage. "I met Cullington at White's and we became involved in a game of faro. When it became very late Cullington offered to put me up for the night."

33

"Did you win?" He looked at her blankly then, allowing the leather curtain to fall. "At faro?" she prompted.

"A little," he answered with maddening vagueness, and then with a touch of irritation added, "You are unusually inquisitive tonight, Eliza."

"I do beg your pardon," she murmured, looking away.

The carriage came to a halt outside a fine mansion in Portman Square. All windows were ablaze with lights, and as soon as the steps were put down the marquis made haste to get out. There were a good many of their acquaintances arriving too, and the Emberays soon became involved in exchanging greetings with some of them.

Once inside the mansion they were soon parted, being claimed by various acquaintances. It was a familiar gathering, and Eliza was usually at ease, but on this occasion she felt that curious looks were being cast in her direction and they discomforted her. Eliza was also aware that she was the subject of discussions, for when she approached various groups their conversation abruptly ceased. The marquis was his usual charming self, and apparently unaware of the phenomenon, and for once Eliza frequently sought out his company, aware that this too invited a good deal of interest from others.

After a while she became more at ease, telling herself she was being unduly sensitive. There were few enough gentlemen present who did not at some time stay out all night, or be seen driving with some flamboyant Cyprian in their carriage. Such behaviour was not unusual, except for Emberay, who, to her knowledge, had not behaved so outrageously before. He always exercised the utmost discretion, and if he had ever been the subject of gossip none of it had ever reached Eliza's ears.

The dinner went well, and when the gentlemen joined the ladies later their hostess stood up to make an announcement.

"My lords, ladies and gentlemen, we have been especially fortunate tonight to have engaged a special guest for your entertainment and diversion. None other than the great Tarrazi is here to sing for us!''

An audible gasp followed the announcement. Several pairs of eyes focused upon Eliza who felt acutely discomforted, for she hated to contemplate what the looks signified. Her cheeks grew pink and she dare not look at her husband.

While the seating was being arranged Phillida Berriman came sidling up to her. ''La Tarrazi sings like an angel, does she not?''

''I trust it will be a good many years before either of us tests the veracity of that statement,'' Eliza snapped.

The other woman laughed. ''How droll,'' she murmured, fanning herself furiously with her fan as she wandered away.

When the seats were finally arranged Eliza deliberately sat as near to the back as she could contrive. Unfortunately her host insisted that she be given a seat with a better view, and Eliza was obliged to move forward.

As Marisa Tarrazi floated into the room in a white muslin gown—the epitome of innocence—she was met by a roar of applause. Eliza had to force herself to clap politely too, aware of numerous pairs of eyes taking in her reaction. For the first time she began to question her husband's involvement with this woman. If the *beau monde*, where such involvements were commonplace, was so much aware of it, then it was likely to be a very serious matter. All at once odd remarks made to her over the past few days by various women took on a new and dreadful meaning.

As La Tarrazi began to sing a Mozart aria, Eliza glanced around the room until she caught sight of her husband. He was leaning against one of the marble pillars, his arms folded in front of him, his eyes never leaving the singer for a moment. He remained there throughout the lengthy performance, and when it was over he was one of the first people to reach the woman with his congratulations. His eyes gleamed and his expression was one of utter joy.

Eliza remained in her seat quite unable to join in the enthusiastic mêlée. She felt heartsick, all the while knowing that if Rosamund Bramwell or Phillida Berriman were in her situation they would carry it off with panache and style, and certainly not sit there wishing to die. Eliza decided nothing greater just then than to be more sophisticated.

"My lady?"

She looked up into the face of a stranger, and a handsome one at that. His fair curls were fashioned *à la Brutus*, and his blue eyes were smiling down on her. "Lieutenant Denzil Peterson at your service, ma'am. I believe you are acquainted with my cousin, Lady Bramwell."

"Oh indeed," she replied, brightening immediately. "I recall her speaking of you on many occasions."

"And she of you."

"I'm delighted to make your acquaintance at last."

"And I yours, my lady, but I have a more pressing reason for inflicting my presence on you. I believe this is yours."

An emerald and diamond bracelet was dangling from his fingers, and Eliza stared at it in astonishment. "Lieutenant Peterson, indeed it is. Where did you find it?"

"It was by your chair in the dining-room, my lady. I was obliged to wait to return it to you until a suitable moment. It is as well you did not miss it earlier. I fear that the catch is faulty."

She took it from him and put it into her reticule. "I am much obliged to you, sir. I shall send it to the jeweller on the morrow."

He bowed. "I hope we shall meet again before too long a time, my lady."

"I am sure we shall," she responded warmly, and he moved away.

Immediately she sought out sight of her husband, only to see him still in rapt conversation with Marisa Tarrazi after many of the others had drifted away. The sight of their intimacy dissipated any pleasure Lieutenant Peterson had created in her.

FIVE

The curtains in Lady Emberay's boudoir were partially closed to shut out the rays of the morning sun, and the marchioness was reclining on a day-bed, a book of poetry open but unread at her side. A sleepless night spent restlessly in her bed thinking over all that had happened the previous evening had left her suffering from a severe headache. During those sleepless hours she had not heard the marquis, who had left the Fullwood's early, return home.

When there came a light knock on the door she did not respond, but even so a few moments later the marquis came in, looking rather hesitant and concerned. He was just about the last person she had wished to see then. Even Horatia with her long face and dire predictions would have been preferable to the man who had caused her so much heartsearching.

"Eliza," he ventured. "Eliza, dear, are you awake?"

"Yes," she answered in a small voice.

He came slowly across the room, peering anxiously through the gloom. "What is ailing you?"

"Nothing to put anyone in a pucker," she responded.

"I met Horatia on the stairs and she told me you had the headache."

"It is much improved now," Eliza replied, swinging

her legs over the side of the day-bed. "There is no cause for alarm."

A faint smile flitted across his lips. "You relieve me, Eliza." He sat down at the end of the day-bed, regarding her sombrely. "I might have known Horatia would make more of it, but it is so unlike you to be at all indisposed. I have never known you take to your bed apart from when you were lying-in."

She smiled faintly. "I have weaknesses just like any other woman."

Despite his solicitude she found herself hating him for the first time in her married life. Even in the early days of their marriage, when he had been a virtual stranger, she had never found cause to dislike him. It seemed so strange that he was unaware of her feeling of humiliation.

"Mayhap I should send for a physician in any event," he told her, still looking doubtful.

"Oh, I beg of you do not. I am almost recovered. The headache is all but gone."

He appeared satisfied then. "It is possible you have overexerted yourself of late. You are to be found here, there and everywhere."

"No more than you," she replied, unable to keep the bitterness out of her voice, something else of which he was not aware.

"You cannot accept every invitation sent to you and hope to keep your health."

She sighed almost imperceptibly. "I'm persuaded you may be correct, Max, and I have thought of going to Brockway for a few days."

"At this time of the year?"

"I received a note from Uncle Frederick this morning. He's been ill."

"Nothing serious, I trust?"

"Just a chill, but I would like to visit him to make certain he is recovered."

"Of course you must. A short period of rustication will be beneficial in any event." She smiled slightly at his eagerness to see her gone from Town. "When do you plan to go?"

"Tomorrow." She looked down at her clenched hands. "My social diary has been rather full of late, but the next few days are not so hectic and there is nothing I cannot cry off."

"Do you wish to take the children?"

"I think not on this occasion. I must return in time for the Bramwell's rout, and it is rather hazardous for children to travel at this time of the year."

He smiled wryly then. "At least if they remain I shall not be left in the sole company of my sister."

"I have no doubt you will not be at a loss for alternative company in my absence."

"Perchance not," he replied, taking out his gold hunter and consulting it.

"You have an appointment," she stated in a dull voice.

He stood up slowly. "If you are not too ill I may as well keep it." He walked across the room and paused by the door. "I am sure we shall see each other before you leave tomorrow."

When he had gone she murmured to herself, "He would go to her if I were on my death-bed."

Then she got up, and walking slowly towards the bell-pull summoned her maid.

The sight of the roaring fire in the library of Brockway Court always reminded Eliza of when she was a little girl, curled up by the hearth with a book in her hand. She was also reminded of the warm sun of Jamaica where she had spent so much time on her father's plantation. At that time she had never dreamed of becoming the Marchioness of Emberay, or anything so grand, although her father admitted on the eve of her wedding he had planned to marry her into the aristocracy from the day of her birth. It had given her quite a jolt to realise her fate had been sealed at such an early age, but she never questioned the rightness of her father's action.

The library was filled with a prodigious number of volumes, and every time Eliza came into it she experienced a sense of wonder, a feeling of an adventure embarked upon, for she had not begun to explore the books it contained. On this occasion, however, the pleasures of her past couldn't have been further from her mind.

"Uncle Frederick," she murmured softly as she closed the door behind her.

"Come along in, my dear," the old man replied from his seat by the roaring fire. He put down the book he'd been reading on the drum-table by his side.

"I wasn't certain you were awake."

"I don't sleep very much these days. Come closer and let me have a look at you."

To Eliza just then he seemed to have aged a good deal since her last visit to Brockway, but she supposed it was natural enough; he was a very old man. He'd had white hair for as long as she could remember, although there was less of it now. He seemed more frail than on previous occasions, and now and again his voice tended to fade away.

"Are you well rested after your journey?" he asked.

"Yes, I thank you, Uncle Frederick."

"Ah, that is a great relief, for you looked unusually hag-ridden when you arrived."

"I am more concerned for you," she reminded him gently. "After all, it is you who has been ill."

"It was only a chill and not a severe one at that. There was no need for you to journey here although I can't be sorry you did."

There was a vestige of his old spirit evident in his eyes, and she smiled. "I'm glad to be here too."

He chuckled. "Let me tell you, it will take more than a chill to put an end to me, Eliza."

"You must not talk of such a thing," she chided. "You have many more years ahead of you."

"Not as many as I have already enjoyed, but I make no protest about that. Life has treated me with the utmost fairness. It is all one can ask."

Eliza was moving about the room, touching fondly remembered objects. "How I love this room," she sighed. "I love this house too. There is nowhere quite like it."

He was frowning, but because she had her back towards him she was not aware of it. "Eliza," he said after a moment, "what is amiss?"

She turned on her heel, laughing. "If you are recovered—and I can see that you are—nothing is amiss."

"I'm flattered and honoured by your concern. I know it is genuine, but I am an old man, Eliza. I was privileged to see you five minutes after you were born, after your sainted mother had breathed her last. You were dear to me at that moment but no less now. I have known you now for two and twenty years, my dear child. There is something amiss and I beg you not to hide it from me." When she averted her face he asked, "Are you increasing again?"

She laughed, albeit harshly. "No, Uncle Frederick, I am not, but if I were it would not trouble me I assure you."

"I had hoped for another great-nephew before I die. You have bonny children, Eliza. I trust they are both well."

"Never better," she answered truthfully. "I shall bring them to see you as usual in the summer."

"Then your concern must be for Emberay." She sighed as she gazed out of the window at naked bushes and skeletal trees. "Is he playing too deep? There is bad blood in the family. I told your father so, but all he could see was the title."

"Max gambles no more than any other gentleman." She went back to the fire and sat down to face her uncle. "You are, of course, correct when you say something is amiss, Uncle Frederick. I cannot hide my unease from you, nor do I wish to."

"So you wish to tell me what troubles you." When she didn't reply he went on, "You can tell me anything you please, Eliza, and I shall always endeavour to do everything in my power to help you."

With great difficulty she said, "There is a female—"

"Ah—" the old man breathed. "I might have guessed. Go on. Tell me what grieves you. It will do you good."

Eliza's voice grew harsh. "There is little to tell, Uncle Frederick. Her name is Marisa Tarrazi."

"How colorful," the old man observed dryly.

"She's an opera singer, all the crack in Town at the moment. The gentlemen of the *ton* are falling over each other for her favours. My husband is among them and is far and away winning the race."

Frederick Derwent smiled and reached out to touch her hand. "Gentlemen of quality are always fancying themselves in love with opera singers, opera dancers, milliners, dressmakers, even maidservants. It is nothing new."

"To me it is, Uncle Frederick, and I don't like it. I'm persuaded everyone is talking about it."

"No doubt they are. It will pass when something new occurs to make the tongues clack."

"Oh, I do pray you are correct. I find it unbearable at present. I don't know which is worse, the tattle or the fact Emberay is in love with this creature."

"Tell me, Eliza, is this the first time Emberay has showed a partiality for another female?"

Eliza got to her feet, smoothing down her neat dimity gown. "Of course not."

42

"Then why are you in such a taking?"

"This is quite different, you see. They have never meant anything to Max or to me before. This time it really is different. I know it is. Signora Tarrazi is no Cyprian or Covent Garden Nun, and my husband is besotted by her."

Her uncle gazed at her for a moment or two before saying, "I have never considered this before, but you must be very much in love with him to be so deeply and unfashionably troubled."

Eliza sat down again and stared at him in astonishment. "Uncle Frederick, I have never thought about it myself before, but it must be so or I wouldn't care so much, would I?"

"My poor little Eliza. I warned your father the marriage he proposed between you two might end in disaster. You were such a green girl and he a rake."

"Up until now our marriage has been very felicitous."

"I'm relieved to hear you say so, but I'm persuaded you were too young. It was wrong to see you married out of the schoolroom. You should have had at least one Season."

"I cannot regret my marriage, but if I'd had a Season it is like I would know better how to cope with this situation."

"No doubt many of your acquaintances already have. The situation you face is not an uncommon one."

"I have imparted many an *on-dit* about other couples," she admitted with a sigh. "I did it so thoughtlessly."

"That will never change, my dear."

Eliza was pensive. "I have never harboured any romantic thoughts about our marriage, however well it turned out. If I'd have been penniless Max would never have looked at me let alone offered marriage, and if he'd had a fortune of his own he would have married some beautiful creature more suited to his style, and I'll warrant he would not, in that event, wish to fall in love with anyone else."

"You do yourself an injustice, my dear. Since your marriage you have acquired poise and confidence, run a number of large establishments with enviable ease, and become an excellent mother. I am very proud of you and I'm persuaded Emberay must be too."

"What use is all that if he does not love me?"

He cast her a wry look. "You never needed that before."

"Only because I never realised I loved him before. I'm not certain you have done me a service in pointing it out."

"I believe you already knew it, Eliza."

She cast him a beseeching look. "Uncle Frederick, what am I to do?"

He sat back in the chair and regarded her sombrely for a moment before clasping his hands together in front of him. "It appears you have two choices before you in this situation. One is to continue as before and allow this woman to have sole claim on your husband's affections for as long as it is like to last."

"That would be too much to bear. My husband is no dilettante. If he is in love with this creature I fear it is a serious matter and will not end so easily or very soon."

"Then the alternative is to fight back, Eliza. You must endeavour to win his love back from her."

Her eyes opened wide. "I cannot conceive how, especially as Max has never loved me."

"Nevertheless you have an advantage not possessed by this other woman. You are his wife and the mother of his children. From all I have observed Emberay is not entirely without feelings for you all. Of course, you are also at a disadvantage too. Wives are tediously familiar creatures who are always there when wanted."

Eliza was forced to smile wryly and her cheeks grew rather pink. "And not very often nowadays, Uncle Frederick."

"Then you must remedy the matter. You must make

him want to be with you in preference to this Signora Parreli.''

"Tarrazi,'' Eliza amended.

"Her name is of no account. I doubt if it is real in any event.''

Eliza's smile faded. "Your advice is no doubt sound, but I wouldn't know how to go about fighting back.''

"Dash it all, Eliza, you're a woman. You must know what is needed to make him take notice of you.''

"You have no notion what our life is like. We have our separate cronies, our different pursuits. When we meet we are polite and felicitous to each other, and now and again he visits my room. I might as well be one of the servants for all he notices. Worse, I could be a piece of furniture.''

"It is up to you to change that situation. Shock him. Surprise him. Act out of character. Take a lover if you must.''

Eliza laughed out loud. "Uncle Frederick, I couldn't.''

"You must. If you are to win your future happiness and peace of mind you must force yourself to do things you have never dreamed about. Show some womanly guile. I know you have it in you.''

She cast him a disbelieving look. "To think I came all this way for such useless advice.''

"It is certainly not useless, and while you are doing all these things, Eliza, make certain you are to be seen as much as possible in this woman's company.''

She almost recoiled at the suggestion. "I couldn't. What good would it do in any event?''

"No doubt this impudent baggage is spectacularly beautiful.'' As Eliza winced he went on, "Well, you, my dear, have hundreds of years of breeding in your blood. When Emberay sees you together he cannot help but be aware of the difference. You are indeed a lady of quality and I assure you it shows.''

Eliza was thoughtful, staring past him out of the window.

"I can only advise you, Eliza," he went on. "It is up to you to decide whether you consider your marriage worth the effort, and if in the end you fail it will not be because you have not tried. And now I suggest you make immediate arrangements to return to London to deal with this matter. As long as you are out of Town this baggage will have it all her own way with your husband."

"I know, but I want to remain here with you for a while longer."

"I'm very tempted to let you, but that will not solve your problem. Go now and give instructions to your servants."

For a moment she did not reply, and then she nodded, getting slowly to her feet. Her uncle followed her progress across the room until she was gone, and then he picked up his book again and began to read.

SIX

Lady Emberay was sitting in her boudoir, replying to some of the many invitations which had arrived in her absence when there came a knock on the door.

Answering her summons a footman entered the room and bowed low. "Lady Bramwell is here to see you, my lady."

Eliza was about to refuse to see her when she realised she could not avoid all of her friends without inviting more tattle than there already was abroad. She sealed the letter and handed it with some others to the lackey. "See that these are despatched without delay and have Lady Bramwell shown up."

As the door closed behind the footman Eliza went to the window which overlooked the courtyard. Sure enough Rosamund Bramwell's barouche was waiting there. The marchioness had no illusions about the reason for her friend's call. She would have heard all the gossip about Emberay and Signora Tarrazi by now and would be curious about Eliza's absence from Town in the middle of the Social Season.

A few minutes later Rosamund Bramwell burst into the room to find a rather subdued and composed marchioness awaiting her. "Eliza, my dear!"

She embraced her friend and then held her away at arm's length. "I wasn't certain you had returned from Brockway and I just wished to ascertain you would be able to attend my rout."

"How could I possibly miss it?" Eliza assured her, leading her friend to a sofa near the fire. "In fact, Madame Poulenc, my dressmaker, is bringing my gown this very morning." Her voice was bright although a trifle brittle. "I trust I have missed no scandals during my absence."

"I think not. Let me see. Ah, yes. I met Eliza Foster only yesterday and she informs me that poor Georgiana Devonshire is gravely ill."

" 'Tis no wonder with her husband's *chère amie* beneath the very same roof. It is more than flesh and blood can stand."

"The arrangement seems to suit."

Eliza was forced to look away from her friend's probing gaze. "I shall call in at Devonshire House at the first opportunity."

"As I understand it the duchess is far too ill to receive visitors. She has very like been given notice to quit."

Eliza was shocked. "I am distressed to hear you say so."

"Speaking of invalids, I was not waylaid by Lady Horatia today. I trust she is not unduly indisposed."

"Oh, much better than that," Eliza replied, brightening again. "She has gone to the country to stay with Emberay's other sister, Dorinda."

"That is a relief for you, Eliza."

"For us all, although," Eliza was quick to add, "Horatia is dear to me. Emberay, however, finds her trying on occasions."

"Indeed, and no wonder. Lady Horatia has a tongue soused in vinegar although I do not doubt she means well. I can fully understand Emberay's inclination to be rid of her just now."

Eliza cast her an innocent look. "Why just now, Rosa?"

Lady Bramwell became uncharacteristically flustered. "I didn't mean—I really—Eliza, it was so odd for you to go away in the middle of the Season. I trust that nothing is amiss. I was most concerned.''

The marchioness laughed. "How foolish of you, Rosa. The reason was a very simple one; Uncle Frederick had been ill and I merely wished to assure myself of his full recovery.''

All the while Eliza avoided looking directly at her friend, who ventured, "Was that your only reason for going?'' For a moment Eliza did not reply, and Rosamund Bramwell went on, "You can rely upon my discretion, my dear. You must know that.''

Eliza sighed. "I am wretchedly unhappy, Rosa. I don't have to tell you why. You have no doubt heard every *on-dit*.''

"You must endeavour not to care, my dear, just as we all do in such circumstances.''

"That is impossible. It is not in me to feign indifference. Has—has Emberay been seeing that woman while I've been away?''

Lady Bramwell hesitated before replying, "He has been observed at the opera house each time she is to sing. Bramwell also reports that Emberay is rarely to be found at his clubs these days, although they were recording wagers on how long the—er—matter would endure.''

Eliza sank back in her seat, staring blankly into space. Rosamund Bramwell asked, "Your Uncle Frederick is the wisest man I have ever known, Eliza. Did he not have any advice to offer?''

"Indeed. He gave me fulsome advice.''

"Well?''

"He suggested that I should turn flirt and shock my husband.''

Lady Bramwell laughed. "I knew one could rely upon Mr. Derwent.''

Eliza stared at her friend in astonishment. "Are you roasting me, Rosa?''

"No indeed. I deem it excellent advice and I suggest you follow it.''

Eliza cast her a look of disgust. "He even instructed me to take a lover."

Lady Bramwell clapped her hands together in delight. "Then you must."

"Faddle! As if I could. His attic's to let if he truly believes I am capable of doing so."

Rosamund Bramwell got to her feet. "I fear you are far too virtuous, more's the pity. However—" she looked at her friend speculatively before clapping her hands together again—"I have just had the most splendid notion." When Eliza looked at her curiously Lady Bramwell went on to explain. "My cousin, Denzil Peterson, is on indefinite leave from the navy and is bored after all the excitement of Trafalgar. He will gladly help, I'm certain."

Eliza was frowning. "Denzil Peterson?"

"My cousin. You do recall him, do you not? Well, he was injured at Trafalgar, not seriously, but he was a while recovering, and then he came up to Town to be diverted, which is something I have not succeeded in doing as yet."

"I do recall I met him at a soirée the other evening a sennight ago. He was very charming, I recall."

"Indeed he is. Handsome, charming, well-connected and something of a hero. He is precisely what we need. I must put it to him without delay."

She began to hurry across the room, and Eliza called, "Don't be in such a fidge, Rosa. You cannot possibly ask Lieutenant Peterson to do such a thing. He will think your attic's to let."

"You may be certain Denzil will agree with me about what is to be done."

Eliza turned away saying irritably, "Oh, it's ludicrous."

Lady Bramwell stood in the centre of the room, her hands on her hips. "Nothing can be more ludicrous than you, my dear Eliza, looking so Friday-faced. It is most unlike you and I am not going to see you mute as a fish while that Italian baggage steals your husband from under your nose. Here," she cast a package at her, "these are the latest fashion plates. I have just collected them. Study them carefully, Eliza, and when you have done so be prepared to act. We shall have that creature all a mort or I've got more hair than wit."

"Rosamund!" Eliza cried in exasperation as the countess whirled out of the room, singing, "Tra-la-la!" in a reasonable facsimile of Marisa Tarrazi.

"She's as mad as May butter," Eliza cried in astonishment, and then against her better judgement opened the package.

As she perused the fashion plates it contained Eliza began to understand how dowdy she had allowed herself to become. Marriage and motherhood had dulled her senses to all the frivolous new fashions. Pretty muslins, Indian cottons and chintz had replaced the heavier materials Eliza usually wore. The latest fashions had an Egyptian look about them, with turbans and feathers which were most becoming.

After a while she put them to one side and stared thoughtfully into space. After some time had passed, still thoughtful, Eliza got to her feet and went to the bell-pull. When the lackey appeared she instructed, "Tell Dorcas to bring my hat and fur-lined pelisse. We're going shopping so I shall require the barouche also."

Having become accustomed of late to his mistress's megrims the footman was surprised to see her in her more normal spirits once again and replied, "It shall be done immediately, my lady."

"Tell Anna to get Lord Aldan ready too," she called after him. "The air will do him good."

Some time later Eliza, her maid, Kit and his nursemaid sallied forth towards Pall Mall and alighted again outside the great emporium of Messrs. Heathstone and Pendlebury. Within the hallowed walls Eliza chose several pieces of cloth, all of which were described as the latest arrivals from the Indies. The materials were quite different to her usual more mundane choices, and if the salesman was surprised by the marchioness's choice he did not make mention of it.

Afterwards the Emberay party went on so Eliza could purchase a selection of ribbons and lace, as well as various coloured feathers for her hair.

"Are we going home now?" Kit asked with an air of someone sorely tried.

"Yes, I think we shall," his mother replied, allowing herself a satisfied sigh. It had been such a long time since she had allowed herself to be so extravagant, but far from feeling guilty about it she experienced only great satisfaction. "Oh no, there is another call I have to make first, dear, but I vow it will not take long."

"After you have done so, may we go to the zoo, Mama?" the boy asked plaintively. "I would like to see all the animals again."

"Why not?" his mother replied. "It will be educational as well as enjoyable."

The carriage came to a halt outside a distinguished-looking jeweller's shop in Bond Street. An escutcheoned chaise was just pulling away when Eliza's carriage stopped. She swept in through the shop door, and as she did so the proprietor and his assistant bowed low and displayed a good deal of pleasure.

"Lady Emberay, this is indeed an honour. How may we serve you?"

"I have called for the bracelet which was brought to you for repair a sennight ago. I'm persuaded it must be ready now."

"It is indeed, my lady." The proprietor snapped his fingers, and moments later his assistant had brought it out of the back room.

"It was only a small repair after all," the jeweller assured her, "and it is quite safe to wear now."

"That is a relief. If it were not for the sharp eyes of a kind gentleman this might well have been lost."

"A tragedy thankfully avoided."

Eliza was about to withdraw when the man ventured, "Your latest commission is ready if you wish to take it now, my lady."

Eliza looked at him blankly. "My latest commission? I'm afraid I don't—"

The man looked immediately abashed. "Oh dear, I do hope Lord Emberay did not intend it as a surprise. I think I am in error in mentioning it."

Eliza walked back towards the counter, her mind in a whirl. "Indeed you are not, sir, and I will take it with me now."

The man appeared to be considerably relieved as his assistant set out a piece of black velvet and placed on it the most exquisite pearl necklace with a detachable diamond drop. The diamond was a large one which winked as it caught the light, making Eliza's eyes swim with tears.

"I am certain your ladyship will consider it a singularly beautiful piece."

"Oh I do," she breathed.

The jeweller looked satisfied. "Lord Emberay was most insistent that it should be the finest diamond and pearls. We were obliged to search carefully which caused some delay, but I think, my lady, you will be delighted with the finished piece."

"It is very beautiful," she said truthfully through a mist of tears.

"Do you wish to take it with you?"

"Yes, I could not possibly leave it now I'm in a fidge to wear it. If my husband calls in today tell him I have taken it with me."

"With pleasure, my lady, but I do not expect his lordship to call until Friday, for I did warn him of the difficulty in locating such fine pearls."

Eliza was scarce able to think properly when she climbed back into the carriage. "Mama, can we go to the zoo now?"

She looked at the boy without really seeing him for a moment or two before replying, "My love, I have just recalled that Madame Poulenc is due to see me, but I vow we shall go to the zoo on another occasion just as soon as it can be arranged."

The disappointment was very evident on his face, and Eliza gathered him close to her. As the carriage set off back to Piccadilly she considered for the first time how closely he favoured his father. Eliza thought she should hate him for that, but, of course, she did not. She kissed him, and he squirmed uncomfortably out of her embrace.

"Why did you do that, Mama?" he asked plaintively, casting her an accusing look.

"Because I love you," she replied, her voice thick with tears.

When they arrived back at Emberay House, Anna hurried her charge back up to the nursery while Eliza removed her bonnet and pelisse.

"Madame Poulenc has arrived, my lady," the house-steward informed her.

She nodded. "I had better go up immediately." She handed her maid the two boxes of jewellery saying, "Take good care of these, Dorcas."

Madame Poulenc was awaiting the marchioness in her dressing-room. The dressmaker quickly waved away Eliza's profuse apologies. "It is my privilege to await your pleasure, my lady. The gown, I believe, is a perfect fit now the final alterations have been made."

When she was fastened into the gown Eliza observed her reflection in the cheval mirror, and what she saw gave her no pleasure.

"Perfect, is it not?" the dressmaker asked with confidence.

"I'm afraid it is not."

The woman's face took on a look of dismay. "My lady, it is just how you wished it to be."

"I am fully aware of that. The error is not yours, madame.

54

However, I would like the bodice cutting much lower at the front.''

"But you never—"

"I do now. I'm not a nun, you know."

"But your ladyship always—"

"Cut it low," Eliza repeated, and then handed her a sheaf of fashion plates. "I also want one each of the gowns marked, madame. The material is being delivered to your establishment directly from Heathstone and Pendlebury."

Madame Poulenc stared in astonishment at the fashion plates and then at Eliza. "My lady, these are not at all in your style."

Eliza stared at her coldly. "I am the one who shall decide upon that. If you feel you cannot execute my orders in this matter I shall be obliged to find someone more willing."

"Oh, my lady, you mistake my concern. I can, of course, make any gown you wish and far better than any other dressmaker in Town."

Eliza smiled at last. "Excellent, Madame Poulenc, and I do trust that the alterations to this one can be completed for tomorrow. I wish to wear it then."

"Certainly, my lady, but the décolleté—if you are absolutely certain—"

"I am."

"Very well, my lady. The gown will be ready by tomorrow afternoon."

The woman gathered up the evening-gown and ushering out her speechless assistant she curtseyed. When they had gone Eliza found Dorcas staring at her strangely.

"Why are you staring at me, Dorcas? Is something amiss?"

"No, my lady. I do beg your pardon."

Eliza drew a sigh as she gazed down at her petticoats. "Fetch my blue velvet. We still have work to do."

"I dread to think what it might be," the maid murmured as she hurried towards the press.

Eliza turned on her heel to look at the woman. "Do you disapprove of my instructions to Madame Poulenc, Dorcas?"

"It's not for the likes of me to say, my lady."

"But do you? You know I value your opinion in such matters. I would be obliged if you'd give it."

Dorcas had been her personal maid ever since she became Marchioness of Emberay, and now Eliza looked at her anxiously. "If my opinion does mean anything, my lady, I think those gowns will look very well on you."

Her words caused Eliza to smile with relief as Dorcas finished fastening the gown. Then Eliza walked purposefully towards the dressing-table, carefully taking all the pins from her hair and allowing it to fall to her shoulders.

"Do you wish to have your hair repinned, my lady," Dorcas enquired, looking puzzled.

"Fetch the scissors, Dorcas."

Again the maid looked taken aback. "Your hair is entirely neat, my lady."

Eliza tapped her fingers against one of the remaining fashion plates. "Only dowds have long hair nowadays, Dorcas. I wish you to cut it short."

The maid's lips moved, but she could not speak. At last she did manage to enquire, "Are you certain you want me to do this, my lady?"

"Quite, quite certain, Dorcas."

As the maid began to snip at the long, dark locks, Eliza sat back in the chair determined now to give Marisa Tarrazi a fight to remember.

SEVEN

"My lady, I declare not even your closest friends will recognise you!" Dorcas declared as she stood back from the dressing-table.

Eliza stared worriedly into the mirror. "Are you certain there is not too much rouge on my lips? My cheeks seem a trifle flushed too."

"You look perfect, my lady. I have never seen you— What jewellery would you have me take out for you?"

"My emer— No, I shall wear the new necklace this evening."

"The one you brought from the jeweller yesterday, my lady?"

Eliza cast her an artless smile. "That is my newest piece unless my husband has been kind enough to bring me another since. I shall also want my pearl bracelets. Bring the Emberay diadem too. That will be sufficient, I fancy."

"Yes, my lady."

A few moments later Dorcas returned with the boxes, and as the maid fastened the new piece of jewellery around her mistress's neck Eliza bit her lip apprehensively, but once it was in place a rage filled her heart, knowing it was undoubtedly meant for another. The splendid Emberay diadem nestled in her new confection of curls, and although Eliza knew she was a match for anyone present that evening, the necklace she wore was a constant reminder that her husband was devoted to another woman.

"There, my lady, that is perfect," Dorcas told her. "You look quite splendid."

"It might have been made for me," Eliza replied in a soft voice.

"It was, wasn't it, my lady?"

Eliza turned to smile at the maid before she got to her feet. "Dorcas, find out if my husband has gone downstairs yet. I shall wait here until he is ready to leave."

The maid curtseyed, leaving Eliza alone in the room. She walked slowly to the cheval mirror and almost timidly raised her eyes. The reflection was practically a stranger with cropped curls which were very much in vogue, carefully painted face and a curvaceous figure in that low-necked satin gown. The gown had turned out to be quite splendid after all, the most fashionable she had ever possessed. Within a matter of days more would be arriving from the dressmaker, all in the very latest vogue. Whatever the outcome of the affair, Eliza knew she would always be pleased with the transformation. She liked her new image very much indeed.

Dorcas came back quietly into the room. "His lordship has just gone down, my lady."

Now that the actual moment had arrived Eliza was suddenly filled with panic. "Oh my goodness. That means I cannot delay any longer."

"Why should you wish to do so, my lady?" the maid asked.

Eliza laughed uneasily. "Why indeed?"

"His lordship seems in a fidge to be gone."

All at once Eliza was despondent. "He is always in a fidge these days."

The maid cast her mistress a pitying glance before picking up her cloak and reticule as Eliza asked anxiously, "Are you quite certain I look—?"

"His lordship will be delighted with your appearance tonight, my lady," the woman told her as she handed over the cloak and reticule. "How can it be otherwise?"

Eliza recalled the necklace she was wearing and could scarcely repress a chuckle. "I wonder."

She took a deep breath before she left the sanctuary of her own rooms and then walked quickly towards the stairs before her courage failed her. She paused on the top stair, for her husband was in the downstairs hall conversing with the house-steward. The marquis was wearing evening-dress, a dark blue coat, white waistcoat and white pantaloons, and as always he looked very handsome. To Eliza there was no one to compare with him and there never had been. Once again she was determined to win his love.

The house-steward's eyes opened wide when he caught sight of his mistress making her way down the stairs. The marquis immediately turned on his heel, saying, "Ah, Eliza, so you're here at—"

The words died in his throat as he stared at her in astonishment. Her heart fluttered nervously as she belatedly wondered if she was making a cake of herself after all.

"Eliza—"

She smiled and appeared unperturbed by his surprise. "Good evening, Max. Are you ready to leave now? I do hope I haven't kept you waiting."

The look of astonishment on his face was all she could have wished for, although she couldn't possibly guess what was behind it. "You look so different," he managed to say at last.

"I trust you do not disapprove," she said with baited breath as she handed her cloak to the house-steward who put it around her shoulders.

"No, indeed I—"

His voice faded away once again as Eliza fastened the cloak, for his gaze had at last alighted on the necklace. For one frightened moment Eliza was afraid her husband might suffer a seizure, and then putting one finger to her throat she smiled coyly.

"Max, you are a dear to try and surprise me with such a splendid gift. I really don't deserve it, you know, but I couldn't have wished for anything better. Only see how it matches my gown. It's as if you knew what I was going to wear."

She stood on her toes and kissed his cheek. "How—how did you get it?" he asked in bewilderment, which his wife found very satisfying. It was not often the Marquis of Emberay was put out of countenance, and certainly not by her.

"When I went to collect my repaired bracelet yesterday, Mr. Jenks asked if I would like to take this with me as it was ready for collection ahead of expectation. You look all a mort, Max. I do hope Mr. Jenks hasn't spoiled your surprise for me. I declare I couldn't be more pleased."

He managed to smile. "That is all which matters. Shall we go?"

He swung his own cape over his shoulders and then ushered her out into the waiting carriage. As it set off in the direction of the Bramwell mansion Eliza drew a profound sigh, aware that he was considering her very carefully and with great perplexity. "You know me so well, my dear. No other man could have chosen jewellery to suit me so perfectly. It's so very flattering. I shall be the envy of every woman there tonight."

He continued to look utterly confounded, but was bound to admit, "It suits you very well, Eliza."

She laughed light-heartedly. "La! A necklace of this beauty and quality would look good on a *sow*." He continued to look uncomfortable as she chattered on, "Dear Rosamund is such a good hostess. I am persuaded her rout will be splendid. Hurricanes of that sort are so enjoyable."

"No doubt you'll wish to remain until very late," he ventured.

"Rosamund would be mortified if I did not."

"I don't believe it necessary for me to remain after supper."

Her eyes widened. "That is quite usual for you, dear, but I would be obliged to stand up for the first cotillion with you."

He was still staring at her in a perplexed fashion, and Eliza dare not contemplate what he might be thinking just then. As she glanced at him speculatively he answered, "Naturally. You may have the first country dance too if you wish."

"Indeed, that would be splendid, Max," she answered with gusto. "I am determined to stand up for every dance this evening if it is at all possible."

He smiled faintly. "You will have no shortage of partners."

"That may well be so, and even if it is, I assure you none dance as well as you, Max. My feet are certain to be crushed by the end of the evening."

"Poor Eliza," he mocked with a vestige of his more customary sarcasm.

"Where—" she ventured, feigning a careless attitude, "do you intend to go later?"

He shrugged his broad shoulders, equally casual. "I am not quite certain. Mayhap Brooks's or White's. Brummell is certain to be there and we can game together for a while. It is always easy to part Brummell from his purse."

"Shame on you," Eliza chided, but behind her apparent levity there was a good deal of concern.

They joined the great many others streaming into Bramwell House. Music drifted down into the street from the ballroom, and passers-by paused to admire the elegant carriages and bejewelled guests who were arriving in a continuous stream along the road. From the moment she entered the handsome marble hall of her friend's home Eliza was aware of speculative glances. This time, however, the attention was welcome.

When they reached the head of the stairs where the earl and countess were greeting their guests, Lord Bramwell eyed Eliza with an unusual amount of appreciation and kissed her hand.

"My dear Lady Emberay, you look absolutely ravishing this evening."

Unused to such fulsome praise Eliza's cheeks grew pink as Lady Bramwell looked on with evident pleasure. "Well done, my dear," she whispered.

As soon as she was afforded the opportunity to do so, the countess took Eliza on one side. "My dear, I know I entreated you to become more fashionable, but I never envisaged that you would actually become a high flyer so quickly."

Eliza looked uncertain. "Do I really look better than I did, Rosa? I beg of you tell me the truth as a bosom friend."

"My dear, have I not already done so? The transformation is remarkable. You look quite another person." When she caught sight of the marquis approaching, she whispered, "We shall have a coze at a more convenient time."

When Eliza danced the cotillion with her husband she held her head up high, even though she was aware there were those who were sniggering behind their fans and talking of Lord Emberay's relationship with La Tarrazi. Many of those who were delightedly gossiping about the affair had husbands who were at that very moment flirting with another lady and drawing them to some quiet part of the house or garden. However, that was no consolation to Eliza.

She was breathless when the lively dance ended, and not merely from the exertion involved. The marquis escorted her to the edge of the dance-floor without speaking a word, and with a sinking heart Eliza detected he was anxious to be gone from the gathering. It did her spirits no good at all to espy Phillida Berriman approaching through the crowds.

The marquis caught sight of her too and drew in a sharp breath before muttering, "That confounded woman. I cannot conceive how she became an acquaintance of yours, Eliza. You have far too much common sense."

Eliza's eyes opened wide at this condemnation, for he had never criticised any of her friends before. "Phillida and I are of a similar age and we embarked upon our married lives at about the same time. We have much in common."

"Eliza! Lord Emberay," the woman greeted them. "How splendid you both look, in such high feather this evening, and you made such an appealing pair in the cotillion. I could scarce take my eyes from you, for you're so rarely to be seen together of late. It truly did my heart good to witness your felicity."

The marquis inclined his head abruptly in answer to her greeting, and all the while she chattered on he eyed her coldly, although she seemed quite unabashed by it. "Don't tell us you were obliged to sit out the cotillion, Mrs. Berriman," he said when she was finally silent.

She laughed uncertainly. "Oh, I cannot stand up for every set, Lord Emberay."

"No indeed," he answered grimly. "You may miss some item of interest if you do."

The woman looked slightly miffed by his sarcasm, but then her eyes widened.

"Is that a new necklace, Eliza? I declare I have not seen it before and it is very fine."

At last Eliza was able to smile quite genuinely although she dare not steal a glance at her husband's face. "It is a gift from Emberay."

Mrs. Berriman glanced at him coyly from behind her lace fan. "La! If Berriman were to buy me such a magnificent piece of jewellery I would be bound to wonder what he had done to warrant it."

Such an allusion could only make Eliza's cheeks flame, but the marquis was unperturbed as he replied, "If I were Berriman you would do well to wonder."

Again Mrs. Berriman was not at all put out by the irony of his reply as she glanced past them. "Here comes Maldon to claim me for the country dance, so please excuse me. Pity my poor feet," she added as she hurried away.

"I pity Clarence Maldon," the marquis murmured as he stared after her darkly.

"Phillida is not as bad as she seems," Eliza was quick to point out.

The marquis looked angry despite an outward calm. Eliza knew the signs so very well. "Women like Mrs. Berriman can cause untold trouble."

"I can think of those who are far more dangerous," she retorted.

He stared at her questioningly, but before he could make any comment someone called her name. Eliza turned as did the marquis to see Lieutenant Peterson approaching them. Eliza recalled him immediately and smiled with a little uncertainty.

The young man bowed low. "Lady Emberay. My lord." He glanced at her anxiously. "It is possible you do not remember me, my lady."

She smiled warmly. "I could not forget the service you did me, sir." She glanced at her husband who still looked angry. "Max, allow me to introduce Lieutenant Peterson of *HMS Courageous*."

"I am deeply honoured to make your acquaintance, my lord," the young man told him, displaying a good deal of charm.

However, the marquis appeared unmoved by it as he

eyed the young man coldly. Eliza explained their previous meeting at the Fullwood's, the recollection of which still pained her. "Lieutenant Peterson was kind enough to retrieve the bracelet which I have just collected from the jeweller."

Throughout the explanation the marquis's face grew progressively darker, and Eliza knew the reason for it all too well. If it hadn't been for Lieutenant Peterson's astute behaviour at the Fullwood's, she would never have discovered the necklace which was intended for Marisa Tarrazi.

"Like my wife, Peterson, I am indebted to you," he said at last, with no such gratitude evident in his manner.

He nodded curtly to them both. "By your leave, Peterson, Eliza," and hurried away, watched by Eliza who drew a small sigh before she turned once again to the other man who immediately asked, "May I have the honour of standing up with you for the country dance?"

Knowing that her husband would have forgotten entirely his promise to dance that too with her, Eliza inclined her head. "That will be a pleasure, Lieutenant Peterson."

He danced well without once stepping on her toes, and Eliza found herself enjoying the glances she was attracting, this time because she was being partnered by a dashing naval lieutenant.

After the dance was ended Eliza was ready to leave his company when he said, "Lady Emberay, supper is being served. Will you allow me to procure some for you?"

Flustered by such unaccustomed attention she could only nod. She supposed her improved appearance must be making a difference, although her husband didn't seem very much impressed by it. Lieutenant Peterson found her a seat in the crowded supper-room and then went to fetch some food.

Eliza watched him curiously. He was a fine-looking young man, although not quite so handsome or as tall as her husband. He did, however, cut quite a dashing figure, and several débutantes giggled behind their fans and chattered excitedly when he passed.

Lord Maldon called out to her, "Save the minuet for me, Lady Emberay."

She nodded and suddenly became aware that her husband was in the supper-room too, something which surprised her, for she had believed him gone. Lieutenant Peterson handed her a plate piled high with tempting morsels of food and then sat down at her side. Lord Emberay was casting them frequent glances despite being engaged in an apparently earnest conversation by Lady Bramwell.

"Lady Emberay," the lieutenant said in a low urgent tone, "I believe it would be beneficial for us to talk now."

"Talk about what, Lieutenant Peterson?" Eliza responded, still watching the marquis, her food untouched on the plate.

"Forgive me— The unfortunate situation in which you find yourself." The young man now had her undivided attention as she turned to stare at him. He smiled faintly. "My cousin explained something of your dilemma to me, and I trust you will forgive her presumption."

Eliza looked away in dismay. "There are few who are not aware of it, but I am always dismayed to learn of it being discussed so freely."

"My cousin is concerned only for your happiness. She is a true friend, you must believe that." When she made no reply, he added, "You may rely upon our discretion, my lady. I admire you greatly and have done so for many years."

Again she looked at him. "I do not recall ever meeting you before."

"That is my loss, my lady. We did meet on several occasions before your marriage, not long after you returned from the Indies. That is of no account now. What is more important is for you to believe I can be of assistance to you now and I would be most honoured if you would allow it."

"I really cannot see how anything you are like to do can help in what is, after all, a commonplace situation."

"I believe my cousin did suggest a way."

Eliza put down her plate at last. "Rosa has windmills in her head."

"On the contrary, my cousin has a good deal of sense. I have always admired it in her. If you decided to allow me to help you I would be most honoured, my lady."

Eliza eyed him steadily, and he did not flinch away from so direct a gaze. "Do you really believe becoming my lover will solve my problem, Lieutenant Peterson?"

He smiled. "Oh, if only it were possible, but my cousin has explained your fondness for the man to whom you are wed. I am of the opinion an appearance of intimacy is all that is required to bring him to his senses."

Eliza stared at him, looking considerably perplexed. "Lieutenant Peterson, how can you possibly gain by such an act?"

"I would find it very gratifying to see you happy, my lady. That is all I hope to gain, apart from the pleasure of your company which you will be obliged to grant me."

Eliza continued to stare at him for a moment, and she knew then he was being sincere, something which made her eyes flood with unbidden tears. "Your kindness is overwhelming, but I cannot allow you—"

"It is my wish, my lady, to be of service to you in any way possible, although I firmly believe any man who behaves in such a cavalier fashion is not worthy of your affection."

"Let me make myself clear, Lieutenant Peterson, I will not allow you to malign my husband. I do hope you understand that."

"I beg your pardon most sincerely, my lady. I vow it shall not occur again."

"I accept your assurance."

"And my assistance?"

"I have no notion how we may go about the matter."

"First of all, allow me to take you riding in the Park tomorrow afternoon."

She looked away from him, experiencing a variety of emotions, none of which were very clear. "I have promised my son I will take him to the zoo on the morrow."

"The day after, then." Eliza glanced at him, her uncertainty still very evident. "What can you possibly lose by merely riding with me?"

After a moment or two she answered breathlessly, "Thank you, Lieutenant Peterson, I shall look forward to it with pleasure."

His eyes met and held hers. "No more than I, my lady."

He took her hand and raised it to his lips. As he did so she glanced across the room. The marquis was staring at them with no expression evident upon his face. After a moment or two he turned on his heel and strode out of the room.

"We will begin immediately," Lieutenant Peterson was saying. "This evening reserve as many dances for me as possible. That is certain to set the tattle boxes chattering, and you may be certain my cousin will be foremost among them."

Eliza smiled her agreement, but as she did so a tide of hopelessness washed over her.

EIGHT

"Mama, that bear is so big," Kit cried, wide-eyed as he strolled around the zoo.

" 'Tis truly amazing," Eliza agreed, relishing his delight in all he saw. "Who would imagine such creatures exist?"

"Have you ever seen anything so ferocious as the tigers?"

Eliza laughed. Nowadays she rarely did so with such spontaneity. "I knew a lady who kept one on a long gold chain in her boudoir."

Kit looked at her in astonishment. "Really, Mama?"

"Yes, really. Her name was Lady Hardwicke and she also kept a monkey."

"Mrs. Berriman has one of those."

Eliza frowned. "I do not recall ever seeing one in her house, Kit."

"I heard Papa saying she has one, called her husband."

Eliza gasped, trying to hide her amusement, as was Anna, walking beside them. "Oh, Kit, dear, you must not say so."

The child was wide-eyed again. "I did not. Papa did. What happened to the lady with the tiger?"

"It ate her, poor thing."

Kit began to jump up and down. "Is that true, Mama? Really, is it so?"

Eliza laughed again. "Well, it very nearly was. She was

69

obliged to give it to the zoo, otherwise it might well have had her for dinner.''

''You don't think one of those might get out and eat us, do you, Mama?'' the child asked, gripping her hand more tightly.

''I shouldn't think so, dear. The cages look quite safe. You're not afraid, are you?''

''No, but it is just as well we didn't bring Lucy with us. She would have been very afraid. Girls always are.''

Eliza was gazing at him indulgently when she caught sight of a couple strolling in the opposite direction. The man was Sir Hugo Nuncton, a hell-raiser of very dubious morals, and the woman was none other than Marisa Tarrazi. She walked along, twirling her parasol, laughing at whatever the man was saying to her.

For a moment Eliza froze in her tracks. She was very much tempted to turn and hurry away in the opposite direction, but after a moment or two she straightened up, gripped Kit's hand and walked purposefully towards them.

When they were abreast Eliza paused. The other woman glanced at her curiously as Eliza nodded to Sir Hugo. ''Good afternoon to you, sir.''

He bowed low, perhaps to hide a malicious smile. ''Lady Emberay.''

Marisa Tarrazi's eyes grew wider, and Eliza smiled at her. ''Signora Tarrazi, is it not?'' The woman, as an afterthought, bobbed a brief curtsey. ''You do not know me, but I am a great admirer of your voice. Such beauty of pitch is so rare.''

The woman looked distinctly discomforted, and Sir Hugo cleared his throat slightly. ''Lady Emberay, you are too kind,'' the singer responded at last, recovering from her dismay.

This time Eliza was delighted she had possessed the advantage of surprise. ''My husband is also a great admirer of yours. In fact he insists upon visiting the opera house as often as our social calendar permits, which is not as often as we should like." She paused before venturing, "You are acquainted with the Marquis of Emberay, I take it."

"We have met," the woman answered in a strangled voice, glancing appealingly at her escort. "He is very condescending."

"I do not doubt it. My husband is not in the least toplofty. Allow me to present our son, Lord Aldan. Kit," his mother reminded him without taking her eyes off Signora Tarrazi.

The child had been staring unashamedly at the other woman, and at his mother's prompting removed his cap and murmured, "How do you do, ma'am?"

"He—is a fine boy," the singer responded, staring at the boy as curiously as the child had been regarding her a moment earlier. "He favours his father, I believe."

Eliza affected astonishment. "How odd you should notice, Signora Tarrazi, but it is undoubtedly true. We are exceeding proud of him as you may well imagine." Eliza smiled from one to the other. "Good day, Signora Tarrazi. Sir Hugo."

The baronet tipped his hat, and Eliza moved on. Far from feeling triumphant she was now trembling, for Signora Tarrazi had never looked lovelier. Love fulfilled must be the finest beauty treatment, Eliza thought as she hurried her son into the waiting carriage without so much as a glance behind her.

She sank back into the squabs as the carriage jerked into movement. Her eyes were bleak as she asked, "Did you enjoy our visit to the zoo, Kit?"

"Yes, indeed I did, Mama, but I did not like that lady. She has an exceeding odd way of speaking."

Eliza cast him an indulgent smile and resisted the impulse to hug him close. "Kit, you mustn't be so scornful. It is only because she is Italian."

"No, she ain't," Dorcas proclaimed, her lips tight with disapproval.

"I beg your pardon," Eliza demanded, taken aback by the unwarranted interruption.

"She ain't Italian, my lady."

Eliza continued to look bewildered. "What on earth do you mean, Dorcas? Of course she's Italian."

"I do beg your pardon, my lady, but her name's Mary Tate and she comes from Wandsworth."

The marchioness continued to look disbelieving. "I think you are mistaken, Dorcas. On what do you base such an accusation?"

"Arthur told me, 'cos he was born in the same building. He's known her for years."

Eliza sat forward in the seat, frowning slightly. "*Who* is Arthur?"

"He's the third footman," Kit supplied, looking pleased with himself. "He can bowl a hoop for *ever*."

A telling flush had spread up the girl's cheeks, and Eliza sat back in the squabs once again, recalling the rather thin and pale young man. "Is Arthur absolutely certain of his facts?"

"Oh yes, my lady. He's got no doubt at all. She's Mary Tate all right. It's a lark, ain't it?"

"Does Arthur also know anything about the Italian nobleman this woman is supposed to have married?"

Dorcas's lips curved into a contemptuous sneer. "She never married any Quality, my lady. It's just a Banbury Tale. Her husband's name was Billy Tate and he was a costermonger at Billingsgate. He was a rotten old mort too, by all accounts."

Her mistress looked hopeful. "Is this man still alive?"

"No. One thing is true; she is a widow. Billy Tate fell into the Fleet one night after drinking a pint of gin."

"I see," Eliza said thoughtfully as the carriage turned into Piccadilly. "Does your knowledge include information as to any offspring she might have?"

"At least one, Arthur says. A boy, he was. He'd be about seven years now, Arthur reckons."

Eliza was still thoughtful as she stared out of the window. "No doubt he is being cared for in some respectable household out of Town."

"It's a real shame the way she's acting so top-lofty in her rum rigging. Putting one in a bag with all those fine gentlemen. It's not right."

When Eliza went into the house she immediately requested Arthur to be sent to her drawing-room.

"I do trust that Arthur has done nothing amiss, my lady," the house-steward enquired.

"Oh, quite the contrary, Raines," Eliza assured him. "I am exceeding pleased with him."

Several minutes later the young man was facing his mistress across her escritoire at which she was sitting. "Dorcas tells me you know something about Signora Tarrazi, the opera singer."

He smiled crookedly. "Yes, my lady."

"Are you absolutely certain she is your old childhood acquaintance? In truth I find it quite an astonishing claim."

"I wasn't sure at first, my lady, what with her fancy name and all, but when she first came to London—as Marisa Tarrazi that is—I accompanied his lordship to the opera, and that's when I saw her. During the interval I slipped down to make sure it was Mary. That was before his lord—"

"And was it Mrs. Tate?" Eliza asked quickly.

"Yes, my lady, it was Mary Tate all right. No doubt of it."

"Did she recognise you, Arthur?"

"Yes, my lady, right away. She was none too pleased to see me I can tell you. Told me to hold my jaw and tipped me a generous vail to do so."

"And did you?"

"Yes, my lady, except for telling Dorcas." He looked all at once bashful. "She's by way of being a friend."

After a moment's consideration Eliza pulled out a drawer in the escritoire, brought out a guinea and gave it to him. "I would be obliged if you remained silent on the matter for the time being, Arthur. Don't discuss it with anyone else, will you?"

"No, my lady, I won't do that, but I may as well tell you

now I'm not the only one to know her. Those buildings are rabbit warrens, and Mary often used too sing for her supper when her old man took all the blunt for gin."

Eliza smiled reassuringly. "That is of no matter." She paused before asking, "Have you any notion where her child might be?"

"No, my lady. He was but a babe when I last heard of her."

Eliza nodded. "I am obliged to you, Arthur."

He bowed low and backed out of the room, leaving Eliza to consider how best to use the unexpectedly enlightening information.

The Marquis of Emberay paced impatiently to and fro even though there was little room to move in the small drawing-room. Now and again he paused to consult his gold pocket watch. Peddlars in the street outside, calling their various wares caused him to go to the window from time to time, only to draw back again moments later. Likewise the sound of an approaching carriage sent him to the window too, only to be disappointed when it drove past.

After a while, when he hurried towards the window again, he was rewarded by the sight of a carriage drawing to a halt just behind his own. Lord Emberay recognised Sir Hugo Nuncton as he handed Marisa Tarrazi down from the curricle. The marquis's heart filled with jealousy and rage, and he was obliged to watch impotently as Sir Hugo raised her hands to his lips while she blushed appealingly.

After what seemed to be an age she left him and came into the house alone. When she entered the drawing-room she pulled off her hat and threw it onto a chair.

"*Caro!*" she greeted him gaily. "What a pleasure."

The marquis's expression did not soften as so often it did when he looked at her. "Marisa, I have been waiting here an unconscionable time."

For a moment she appeared concerned, and then she shrugged. "I beg your pardon, my lord. Sir Hugo took me to the zoo and we were so diverted by what we saw there I forgot the time entirely.''

''You forgot I was going to be here?''

She smiled and went to take his hands in hers, looking up into his face. ''*Caro*, your anger wounds me deeply, so I beg of you say you forgive me.''

''I can forgive you anything, Marisa, but I am so madly in love with you I cannot bear to think of you in the arms of any other man.''

''If that is truly so, just imagine how I feel when you return to your wife.''

He looked even more irritated as he drew away from her. ''You must not torture yourself on that score. Eliza and I are on cordial terms, but no more than that. Marisa, you must vow to me that there is no one else in your life for whom you truly care.''

''I have done so on many an occasion, *caro*, but if you wish it I tell you again. You are my only love.''

''And yet you accept the company of other gentlemen, and gladly from all I observe.''

''Why should I not?'' she asked with a shrug.

''Because it displeases me.''

She looked coy. ''That is a remarkably unfashionable attitude for a man of your style.''

''Oh, faddle to that, Marisa,'' he responded, not trying to hide his irritation.

She laughed maddeningly. ''Be assured those gentlemen mean no more to me than your wife does to you.''

She walked away from him, and he went to her, putting his hands on her shoulders. ''We have wasted enough time, so let us not quarrel.''

''What would you have us do?'' she asked archly, still keeping her back towards him.

''Come with me for a ride in the Park. I want you at my side for the entire world to see.''

"What will that signify? Wagers will be won or lost. It is nothing."

He frowned. "Marisa, what is troubling you? You are in an odd mood today."

She smiled faintly, glancing up at him. "I am merely tired. It is growing late and I must practice my scales. My voice is not a machine."

He made a noise of impatience. "You do not need to exhaust yourself singing. I want to provide for your every need which will be my privilege and my pleasure. You *must* allow me to buy you an establishment of your own."

"I shall see you no more often than I do now," she answered wistfully.

"I am of the opinion we meet very often, Marisa."

"I cannot accept your offer, generous as it is," she said in a broken voice a moment later. "I don't wish to be hidden away from the world, seeing you only when your appointments permit."

His hands dropped to his sides. "You know very well I cannot marry you, Marisa."

"I try not to think about it, because you are the only man I shall ever love. How I long for the right to stand at your side for all the world to see, to bear your children, and I know you want it too. That is why I seek diversions where I may, enjoy the adulation of others, because in my heart I am desolate. I am the toast of the Town and yet what I really want, true happiness, can never be mine."

He listened to her in silence before putting his arms around her waist. "My dearest Marisa, I cannot bear to hear you voice your unhappiness. It tears at my heart."

She turned round to face him, smiling then, "But I also know so much happiness with you, my love, so much happiness. I can hardly bear it."

"That is nothing to the happiness we will share in the future," he promised.

"Shall we?" she asked, searching his face beseechingly. Then she moved away.

"What is really troubling you?"

"I saw your wife and son at the zoo today." He looked startled. "I curtseyed to her. She was exceeding condescending to me, but I realised then that I was nothing, nothing at all."

"You are everything to me."

"If only we could declare that to the world, *caro*," she said softly.

His eyes met hers soberly. "You know what you are asking, Marisa?"

"I ask only to serve you all my days, to be your adoring slave."

He looked away, drawing a sigh. "You must give me time to ponder on this matter."

Her eyes grew wide with dismay. "*Caro*, you must not think of it at all. I admire Lady Emberay so much. I care for your happiness above my own. You have a fine son and a daughter to consider above me. How I wish they were mine."

He smiled faintly. "You do realise that Kit will remain my heir whatever happens in the future."

"I care only for the right to be with you, my dear love."

He drew a sigh, looking away from her again. "There is a way to fulfill our happiness, and I am determined to find it."

Marisa Tarrazi remained motionless in the centre of the room until she heard the front door close behind the marquis, and then her doleful expression gave way to a smile. When her maidservant entered the room a short while later she found her mistress laughing merrily.

"Signora?"

"You had better start to practise calling me my lady. Emberay will come up to scratch yet. Oh, Mimsie, if only you'd seen me just now. I declare I am a greater actress than a singer. Greater even than Sarah Siddons. I know she could not have done better!"

NINE

"Would you care to tool the ribbons, Lady Emberay?" Lieutenant Peterson enquired as he drove his curricle into Hyde Park at the fashionable hour.

The paths were crowded with both carriages and pedestrians, making progress slow, and Eliza's companion was noted by many of her acquaintances, which was in fact the purpose of their drive. Quizzing-glasses were raised as the curricle passed by, and Eliza feigned an air of nonchalance although the outing had filled her with dread and she was still ill at ease. One of the reasons for her discomfort was a distinct feeling that Lieutenant Peterson was less indifferent to her than she would have liked. However, as the gentleman had said, she had very little to lose, and the number of society ladies of her acquaintance who actually did have lovers were legion.

"I warn you I am an excellent driver," she told him as she took the reins. "My husband taught me when we were on our honeymoon." Her eyes darkened suddenly. "How long ago that was."

"You could have no better teacher." She cast him a curious look, and he went on quickly, "I am a great admirer of Lord Emberay's prowess in various fields. In fact, I was privileged to watch him give Nuncton a good milling at Gentleman Jackson's only yesterday."

The marchioness looked at him again. "My husband is a true Corinthian, and I suppose you must wonder why he married a dowd like me."

"A dowd!" he exclaimed, laughing at the same time. He raised his hat to a passing horseman, and Eliza nodded to a group of acquaintances. "Lady Emberay, you are one of the most stylish and beautiful women I have ever clapped eyes upon."

So surprised was she, Eliza almost pulled the horses to a standstill. They whinnied angrily as she declared, "You are roasting me, Lieutenant Peterson."

"I assure you I do not."

Embarrassed by his evident sincerity she urged on the horses once again. "Your opinion is coloured by my unfortunate situation."

"Not so much I cannot tell diamonds from glass, and I fear your husband is a buffle-head if he prefers that woman to you."

"Lieutenant Peterson, you vowed you would not malign my husband."

"So I did. Beg your pardon, my lady."

She cast him a beseeching look. "If you are genuine in your admiration for me—"

"You must know that I am."

"Then the consequence of what you are doing might well go against what you truly wish."

He smiled faintly. "As I told you the other evening, your happiness is of the greatest import to me. I hope and pray you will achieve what you desire, but in the event you do not, mayhap you will allow me to ease your pain."

She looked away in embarrassment. "I cannot envisage my future," she told him bleakly.

"I would not expect you to do so."

They drove on in silence for a while, and Eliza was still thoughtful. She couldn't truly envisage life without the marquis no more than she could imagine allowing herself to be consoled for his loss by this very charming and handsome man.

"How fetching you look of late," a voice called out to her.

Eliza jerked out of her thoughts to see Phillida Berriman driving alongside in her own gig. Eliza smiled, appearing outwardly carefree. "Thank you, Phillida dear. Your opinion means so much to me."

The woman then transferred her attention to Eliza's companion. "Good day to you, Lieutenant Peterson. I note that the war rages on without you."

"Good day, Mrs. Berriman," he answered with a smile. "I am afraid I could not persuade Boney to postpone the fighting until I am fit enough to rejoin my ship."

Mrs. Berriman affected an air of astonishment. "For a wounded man you contrive very well, my dear." Then she transferred her attention back to Eliza. "I do not suppose you would be willing to confide in me where you obtained that delightful hat."

"It would be of no use if I did, Phillida. My milliner has a dozen duchesses as clients. She was reluctant enough to take on a mere marchioness."

If the woman was piqued she did not show it. She merely laughed, flicked her whip over the back of her horse and with a wave drove on.

"My goodness," Eliza cried, "that is the first time anyone has wanted to know where I obtained my hats."

"I have noted that many ladies had admired it since we drove into the Park."

Eliza cast him a laughing look. "Oh, I'm persuaded that is because they admire my companion rather than my hat."

She was about to urge on the team when Lieutenant Peterson took back the reins. A moment later Eliza realised why; a short distance away the marquis, with La Tarrazi at his side, was driving towards them and eliciting a good deal of attention.

Eliza was suddenly panic-stricken, something of which Denzil Peterson must have been immediately aware, for he whispered, "Lady Emberay, I am at your side. It is most important that you affect an air of unconcern."

"I cannot," she gasped. "It is difficult enough to encounter that woman when she is not with my husband. Pray turn the carriage around. There is still time to evade them."

"Look at me," he ordered, and she did so, wide-eyed and fearful. "Now, imagine Lord Emberay is driving along with—an ape at his side."

The notion immediately caused Eliza to burst out laughing. "Lieutenant Peterson, you are outrageous."

The marquis slowed his high-perch phaeton when he caught sight of his wife driving along in the company of the dashing lieutenant. She was laughing at something he had said, after gazing longingly into his eyes. Lord Emberay had the feeling he was seeing a side of his wife he had never noticed before, and the realisation shocked him.

"Emberay, is that not your wife over there?" Marisa Tarrazi asked after a moment.

"I believe it is," he answered lightly.

"Surely you must know."

"Yes, it is Eliza," he answered, looking vexed.

"I thought it must be. How charming she looks."

"Yes, doesn't she?" he replied with no evident pleasure.

"Her hat is quite adorable."

"It looks exceeding frivolous to me."

"You cannot fully appreciate such matters, no more than I understand the importance of a certain fold of the neckcloth."

"That is quite a different matter," he told her severely.

"And who is the gentleman at her side?"

"A Lieutenant Denzil Peterson, a cousin of the Countess of Bramwell."

"They appear to be on intimate terms, *caro*. I thought you said your wife did not have a lover."

"She hasn't," he snapped. "The notion is utterly ludicrous."

Marisa Tarrazi laughed. "I think you are mistaken. Their relationship is very evident to me, but mayhap we ladies have more of an instinct in these matters."

The two carriages were almost abreast. Eliza's eyes glowed. "Emberay. Signora Tarrazi, what a pleasant occurrence." The marquis and Lieutenant Peterson nodded to each other as Eliza went on eagerly, "Allow me to introduce Lieutenant Peterson, Signora Tarrazi."

The young man tipped his high-crowned beaver hat. "Signora, what a pleasure it is to make your acquaintance at last. I have heard so much about you of late."

"Only good things, I trust," she replied.

Lieutenant Peterson laughed. "Signora Tarrazi, there are those who would find fault with a fat goose, but I am a man who prefers to make up his own mind."

"That is something I always admire in a man. You must come to see me at the theatre and you will be obliged to agree I am the greatest singer alive."

"I shall look forward to it, signora."

All the while Eliza and her husband were exchanging icy looks. Then the marquis said, "It seems we are causing some congestion by dallying here so we shall move on. Eliza. Lieutenant Peterson."

The carriages moved on in the opposite direction, and Eliza drew a profound sigh. "Oh, my goodness, she grows lovelier every time I see her."

"Tush," was his curt reply. "She may be passable at a distance but there is no comparison to you, and as for modesty—well, she really cannot know the meaning of the word."

Eliza smiled and touched his hand. "Dear Lieutenant Peterson, even if I do succeed in wresting his affection from that creature I shall always be grateful to you for helping me through this dreadful time.''

Moving away, the marquis glanced back to see his wife move closer to her companion and touch his hand so tenderly. Marisa Tarrazi did not miss the gesture either, and she looked rather pleased.

"It appears to me as if your wife is cap over heels in love with that very handsome young man, and who can possibly blame her? He is very charming.''

"Does your mind dwell on nothing else?''

"There is nothing else worthwhile to dwell upon as I am persuaded Lady Emberay would agree. It would be foolish of you to believe a lady as beautiful as your wife would remain at home with her sewing while you do exactly as you please.''

He was evidently startled, and she ventured, "At least you know now you need harbour no fears over her well-being and happiness, *caro*. No doubt she would be as relieved as you to be free to be with her lieutenant more often.'' She paused before asking, "Have you given any further thought to our future?''

"A great deal.'' He glanced at her. "I must of course discuss the matter with my wife.''

Marisa Tarrazi smiled. "She will welcome your broaching the subject. Of course, knowing about Lieutenant Peterson changes matters somewhat, wouldn't you agree?''

"I cannot see how,'' he answered irritably.

She smiled with satisfaction. "Only think, *caro*; if you contrive to catch her in a compromising situation with her lover, no blame will attach to you. Is that not much better?''

"There will be none of that, Marisa.'' He looked grim.

Signora Tarrazi's face took on an expression of dismay. "But our future can be settled so much more quickly that way.''

"You need have no fear; the matter will soon be re-solved to everyone's satisfaction."

"How happy we shall be," Marisa Tarrazi crooned.

The marquis flicked his whip over the backs of his team of matched greys which surged forward, almost tossing his companion out of the phaeton. Moments later one hand was clinging to the side for dear life and the other to her hat as the phaeton raced out of the Park and along the Lane beyond.

Eliza pulled her filmy negligee closer about her as the door to her boudoir opened. The marquis stood in the doorway, gazing around, noting the number of new gowns brought by the dressmaker, which were strewn about every avail-able surface. Madame Poulenc and her assistant curtseyed and quickly removed both themselves and the gowns, leav-ing Eliza to face her husband alone.

For once she scarcely knew what to say to him, although she smiled a greeting. He seemed to be little more than a cold stranger of late, whereas once she might have sworn she had known him in all his moods.

As he continued to hesitate in the doorway only the wringing of her hands betrayed her unease. "Max, my dear, how odd it is to see you home at this time of the day."

He eyed her coldly. "The same may be said of you, Eliza."

She laughed, managing to keep up the brittle air. "How true that is. I find life so diverting of late."

"I had noticed," he said, without pleasure.

"Had you? I'm so glad. I know how you loathe Friday-faces about you. Well, do come in. I have finished my fittings now."

He did move further into the room, sniffing derisively. "Eliza, what is that odour?"

The marchioness looked around in alarm, and then her

eyes lighted upon a vase of flowers. "There is the culprit, I'll warrant. A bouquet from Lieutenant Peterson. He knows how I adore violets."

Lord Emberay looked derisive. "And I hate them. They always make me sneeze."

"Dorcas," Eliza called, and when the girl came out of the dressing-room she ordered, "Remove this vase. They are annoying his lordship." The marquis looked mildly satisfied until his wife added, "Put them in my bedchamber. He will not be troubled by them there."

She sat down on a sofa by the fire and appeared entirely at ease. "Do sit down, Max, if you have time to spare. We seem to see so little of each other of late." She patted the seat, and he sat down at the other end of the sofa, removing a gold snuff-box from his pocket and taking a pinch with studied care.

"May we talk for a while?" he asked, returning the box to his pocket.

"What a splendid idea. Only I must go along to Devonshire House to pay my respects to poor Devonshire."

"Georgiana is indeed a great loss," the marquis responded with feeling.

"I wonder if the duke will marry Lady Foster now. Do you think having his paramour under the same roof helped to put an early end to Georgiana?"

"I wouldn't know," he answered, his manner still cold. "From all I could see the duchess and Lady Foster were very close friends."

"The duke might well marry Lady Foster now," Eliza ventured. "If I die would you marry again?"

He looked shocked. "Eliza, you are only two and twenty. It is more like I should get notice to quit first."

"Ah, but life is so uncertain, my dear. Only think of poor Georgiana Devonshire. Lady Foster, however, is eminently suited to looking after the children; after all no one is certain whose belong to whom. I wonder who would make a good mother to Kit and Lucy.''

''No one could be better than you, Eliza.''

She chuckled. ''But what if I were not here?''

He became more alert. ''What do you mean?''

She shrugged. ''It is foolish of me to consider such a matter. I intend to see my great-grandchildren.''

''While we are talking about children,'' he cut in quickly, ''My son informs me that he wishes to join the navy as soon as he is old enough. That is something new, I fancy.''

Eliza laughed gaily. ''Oh dear, I fear that is Lieutenant Peterson's influence.'' The marquis was not pleased, and that was very apparent. ''Kit is easily influenced,'' she added quickly. ''He is such a baby. Naturally, Lucy isn't impressed at all.''

It was his turn to laugh. ''Eliza, Lucy is not yet *three*.''

She laughed again too until she became aware that he was staring at the negligee, and she resisted the temptation to pull it closer about her. ''I haven't seen that garment before,'' he said a moment later.

''Well, I have owned it some considerable time,'' she answered wryly. ''The problem is, my dear, we lead such busy lives.''

''It has come to my notice that you lost two hundred guineas playing faro at Alliot's house the other evening.''

Eliza immediately looked abashed. ''Oh, I do hope you are not intent upon giving me a set-down over that omission.''

''Not at all. I was merely curious, for you have never displayed a desire to gamble before.

She chuckled. ''No, indeed, but so many of our acquaintances derive a good deal of pleasure from gaming, I deemed it worth a try.''

''I trust the costly lesson has satisfied your curiosity on the matter once and for all.''

"Oh no, I enjoyed it immensely. I suppose," she ventured after a pause, "you have also been told that I won a thousand guineas at hazard the following evening." From the look of surprise on his face she knew he had not and she went on quickly, savouring the moment, "By the by, do you intend to visit the opera tonight?"

His look of surprise turned to one of suspicion. "It is always possible. Do you have a particular reason for asking?"

"Yes. You see, La Tarrazi is singing and Lieutenant Peterson has been told so much about her he is in a fidge to see her for himself, so may we join you if you intend to be there?"

He seemed far from pleased, although he replied, "Yes indeed, you will be welcome." After a moment's consideration he said, "You seem to be seeing a good deal of that young man of late, Eliza."

"He's so very persistent, I own," she answered thoughtfully.

"Even so, you evidently enjoy his company."

Eliza was wide-eyed. "He is so amusing, Max. I find his company exceeding diverting."

"He is, I understand, Rosamund Bramwell's cousin. No doubt you have been acquainted some considerable time."

"It would appear he and I knew each other as children. It can be rather odd how childhood acquaintances suddenly reinstate themselves after so many years," she added thoughtfully, and then more cheerfully, "I received a letter from Horatia this morning."

He became more alert. "She is not returning to Town is she, Eliza?"

The marchioness chuckled. "You are positively quaking with fear."

He looked discomforted by her teasing. "Scarcely that, but if I were, is it any wonder?"

"I have never known you to be afraid of anyone before."

"I am not afraid of m'sister!"

She laughed. "Dearest, everyone is just a little afraid of her, or at least in awe of her, so you'll be glad to learn she is remaining for the present with your other sister. The poor dear was all done-up after the journey down to Devon and it seems she needs time to recover her spirits."

"I am considerably relieved to hear it."

"How unfeeling," his wife chided.

"There is nothing wrong with her health, Eliza, and you know it as well as I do. She is healthier and stronger than any of us."

"Ah, but she does not believe that, Max, and it would be very cruel to deprive her of the one thing in which she excels."

He smiled faintly. "Dorinda is far more equipped to cope with her megrims than I am."

Eliza suddenly clapped one hand to her lips. "What a chuckle-head I am. You came to talk to me on some topic of great import, and here I am blabbering on about foolish matters."

He had become more at ease during their conversation, but his sudden look of strain filled her with foreboding. It was so difficult to put on a carefree manner, and doing so was a great strain.

Slowly he got to his feet, drawing himself to full height. "It is of no real import, Eliza. You had better get dressed if you wish to visit Devonshire House. In fact, I have it in mind to accompany you."

Immediately she became troubled. "Oh dear, I do wish I'd known that before. Lieutenant Peterson has obligingly agreed to take me."

A look of anger fleetingly crossed his face. "Very well. In that event we shall all go together." Suddenly he frowned. "This desire of his to go to the opera is very strange; has he not heard Signora Tarrazi sing before?"

"Evidently not."

"I was of the opinion he was present at the Fullwood's that evening when Signora Tarrazi sang."

"Yes, he was present, of course, but I believe he didn't take much note of her that evening."

"I cannot comprehend that."

"Well, 'tis true," Eliza replied lightly.

He walked across to the door before pausing there for a moment. "If you intend to go to the opera tonight you may as well travel there with me. You may tell Lieutenant Peterson to meet us there."

Eliza smiled uncertainly. "Yes, Max, if that is what you wish."

After the door had closed behind him she sank down on the sofa again, running her hands through her hair before jumping up again, throwing off the negligee and dressing as quickly as she could.

TEN

Marisa Tarrazi's performance as Dorabella was superb. Eliza doubted if anyone could dispute it. She had prepared herself with great care for the evening's entertainment. Whenever possible she wore the new pearl necklace which she noted her husband eyed uneasily. She had also chosen to wear one of her new, fashionable gowns, and with matching feathers in her hair Eliza did not need Lieutenant Peterson to tell her she presented a fine figure, but it was to no avail for throughout the first act the marquis sat as if transfixed by the vision before him. When the first act came to an end he immediately got to his feet and began to leave the box.

Almost as an afterthought he paused to look at Eliza, and then addressed Lieutenant Peterson. "Peterson, I'd be obliged if you'd fetch my wife some lemonade. Pray excuse me, for I must congratulate Signora Tarrazi on the superb first act."

It was evident he could scarcely wait to leave them, and Eliza watched him go before the other man asked in a solicitous tone, "Would you like me to procure some refreshment for you, my lady?"

She shook her head sadly, and he moved to a seat closer in the box. Aware that they were being quizzed all around,

Eliza inclined her head towards him almost automatically, although her thoughts were far away.

In almost a whisper Lieutenant Peterson went on, "Lady Emberay, there will be many gentlemen visiting La Tarrazi during the interval."

She drew a deep sigh. "I know that, but I am also aware that this is a hopeless situation. He is as besotted as ever. There is no end to it."

"Be of stout heart, my lady. If he is deeply besotted by that woman we cannot expect him to fall out of love so quickly. You do possess a trump card; you know she is not what she pretends to be."

"I cannot use the knowledge. If I tell Emberay it will make no odds to his feelings for her. He is too infatuated, and moreover she will tell him some Banbury Tale of how she fought her way out of the slums. It might be true, I suppose, but in any event he will admire her even more at the end of it."

"It might well take time to open his eyes to your true worth, but I am persuaded the battle is far from lost."

She smiled at him fondly. "You are a brave man, Lieutenant Peterson. You and men like you won at Trafalgar, but love is not a battleground."

"From all I have observed it is a far bloodier battle than any on land or sea."

"If it were not for you I should have despaired by now."

"Glad to be of service, ma'am," he responded brightly, giving her a mock salute which made her laugh.

It was at this point that the marquis returned. He paused at the entrance to the box, taking in the sight of his wife and her companion, heads close together, laughing like conspirators. For some reason he was angry as he sat down again, casting them both cool glances.

"I trust Signora Tarrazi is in good voice for the second act," Lieutenant Peterson enquired with the utmost concern.

"Never better," the marquis snapped, raising his quizzing-glass and peering at the occupants of a box across the auditorium with great concentration.

"You have not exaggerated her ability in any way," the man went on. "Signora Tarrazi sings like a lark. I am indebted to you for granting me this opportunity to see her in the splendour of your box, my lord."

"Signora Tarrazi makes me feel so inadequate," Eliza confided, and her husband looked at her curiously.

"You would not wish to be a singer, would you, Eliza? I have never noted such a wish before."

She laughed deprecatingly. "It is merely that I have so few accomplishments."

"I believe Lord Emberay would agree you are most accomplished in the matters important to a wife," Lieutenant Peterson answered. "Do you not agree, my lord?"

The marquis turned in his seat to face the young man. "I do indeed."

"I truly envy you your good fortune, my lord."

As the second act commenced Eliza sat back to endure it, for enjoying the performance was beyond her. Sitting through the opera was very painful to her and she wished she might have avoided it. However, Lieutenant Peterson had thought it a good idea to attend, and Eliza acknowledged that he could be far more objective than she.

Lieutenant Peterson was left to escort Eliza home afterwards, and she was unusually quiet in the carriage. "Lord Emberay says he has gone to White's to play whist," the young man ventured after a while. "I am a member too and I have it in mind to go and discover for myself if he is there."

Eliza glanced at him. "You have no need to go to such trouble. I know where he is. He is with La Tarrazi."

Lieutenant Peterson looked vexed. "If only he had a rival, someone to capture her affections. From all I have heard no other buck has succeeded in staying so close to her.''

Eliza laughed harshly. ''Mayhap you would be more profitably engaged in capturing her affections than pretending to vie for mine.''

''I could not convincingly do so, and such an attempt might entrap Lord Emberay more firmly in her clutches. Rivalry is often a great spur. In my opinion that is why he is so infatuated now.''

''He could not be more entrapped than now, whatever anyone does.'' She cast him a curious look. ''How strange this must seem to you, sir.''

He smiled in the darkness. ''It is only strange that Lord Emberay should display such uncharacteristic foolishness, and I do know what it is to love, my lady. It is the most powerful emotion of all.''

Again she looked at him with interest. ''You speak of love so convincingly. Have you never wished to marry?''

''Yes, indeed. That is still a dear wish of mine.''

''Have you ever been tempted?''

''Oh, yes, my lady. I was once madly in love with the most delightful chit.''

For once Eliza forgot her own problems. ''What happened?''

''I was not deemed well enough connected by her family, and the lady—wed another.''

Her eyes filled with pain. ''Did she love you too, Lieutenant Peterson?''

He hesitated before answering with a disarming smile. ''I think not. It was rather a long time ago, before I joined the navy.''

''I really am very sorry to hear your tale. You deserve so much more.''

He laughed. ''I think so too.''

''You must put all thoughts of her from your mind and

allow yourself to fall in love again, but this time with someone who is able to return your devotion."

He drew a sigh. "It is possible, once your affairs are brought to a satisfactory conclusion. I may well seek out a suitable lady."

A shadow crossed her face. "That makes me feel a trifle selfish to monopolise your valuable time."

"You did not force me into this ruse, my lady, and I am glad enough to enjoy your company for the time being. I confess you protect me from a legion of matchmaking Mamas whose daughters do not interest me one bit."

Eliza laughed then. "If that is so then let us consign my husband and his doxy to the devil for the rest of the evening and enjoy a conversation devoid of the megrims."

"I heartily concur, Lady Emberay," he replied as the carriage drew up in the courtyard outside Emberay House.

As Lieutenant Peterson helped her alight from the carriage, Eliza wondered if she would be able to consign thoughts of her husband and his love from her mind so easily.

The room was filled with the gentle glow of candlelight. Lord Emberay reached across the table and refilled Marisa Tarrazi's wineglass.

"In a large establishment such as yours," she ventured, lifting the glass to her lips, "I imagine there are servants around all the while and the master and mistress are very rarely afforded an opportunity to be entirely alone like this."

"There are a great many servants at my house," he admitted. "I am rarely obliged to fill my own wineglass, but being alone here with you is so much better, I must own."

"When marriages are arranged for convenience, as so many are, it must be difficult to get to know one's spouse."

He smiled faintly in the candlelight. "I am beginning to realise that is so often the case."

She glanced around her before drawing a profound sigh. "This room must seem very poor to you, *caro*, after the grand houses you are accustomed to."

"Just now I would not wish to be anywhere but here. This is the finest place in the world—where you are."

She smiled with satisfaction before saying, "I believe I was in better voice than ever tonight. Do you not agree, *caro*?"

He gazed across the table, the remnants of their ample supper before them. "You were magnificent. There is no one to compare with you. The great Catalini was only great before you arrived in England. My guest, Lieutenant Peterson, was entranced despite his currently inexplicable attachment to my wife."

"Mayhap he too will fall in love with me. But no," she amended regretfully, "I must leave Lady Emberay with some consolation."

The marquis shifted uneasily in his chair before he asked, "Tell me something of your life before I knew you."

It was her turn to look uneasy. "Why do you ask? It is of little interest, I assure you."

The marquis laughed in astonishment. "It must be of interest, for I can never know enough about you, Marisa."

She smiled, leaning across the table. "The past is nothing to me now; the present, the future, is all which matters." She reached out to touch his hand. "I have heard that you and Sir Hugo Nuncton—fought together the other day."

He drained his wineglass and then refilled it. Marisa Tarrazi covered hers. "Oh, it was merely an exercise, my dear. It was nothing more than that, I assure you."

She pouted. "How disappointing, especially as I was told you drew his cork."

"You are remarkably well-informed, but I may as well admit Sir Hugo could easily have drawn *my* cork."

"I do not believe that for one moment, but you are most unchivalrous; I was quite persuaded you and Sir Hugo were fighting over me."

"I am sure neither of us considered it. My elder brother, who inherited the title from my father, was killed in a duel, which I regarded as the height of foolishness. I have dealt with many a buck who was longing to challenge me, but I have always managed to fend them off with no loss of face."

"So you would not fight for me?"

"I doubt if it would ever be necessary, Marisa. You assure me I have no rivals, and if gentlemen wish to pursue you I cannot find it in me to blame them."

"This is a sudden change of heart, *caro*. You have always resented my having other suitors."

"I mind very much indeed." He drained his wineglass yet again. "But I also recognise that I have no right to do so."

"Have you—given any more consideration to our future?" she asked in a slightly breathless voice.

He sat back in the chair and in a leisurely manner took a pinch of snuff. "I have done a great deal of thinking of late," he admitted. "The matter of our relationship is never far from my mind."

"You intimated to me not long ago that you wished to discuss certain matters with Lady Emberay."

He glanced at her quickly and away again. "Oh, indeed I shall, only the opportunity has not presented itself. My wife and I are scarce able to pass the time of day."

Marisa Tarazzi laughed uncertainly. "It is true Lady Emberay is very much involved with Lieutenant Peterson, but this is a matter of the utmost import."

"And therefore not to be embarked upon in a hasty manner."

The singer looked rather pensive. "Mayhap you believe Lady Emberay will be devastated when you speak to her of your love for me, but you may be surprised to discover she is not."

The marquis looked vexed. "I take leave to doubt she will be pleased at the news."

"If she is in a like situation it is possible she will be."

Marisa Tarrazi pushed back her chair, got to her feet and walked across the room, watched all the while by the marquis who replied, "If you refer to Lieutenant Peterson, I had not considered his involvement at all. The truth is, my wife is very much discomposed at the passing of Georgiana Devonshire, and I had not wished to disturb her further at this time."

Marisa Tarazzi pressed her hands together. "Ah yes, the beautiful duchess. I fear that the *beau monde* will not be the same without her." She turned to look at him. "However, it is like that the duke will now marry his true love."

The marquis smiled faintly in the candlelight. "That is by no means certain. Devonshire will first be obliged to pay all his late wife's debts, which are considerable."

He took out his pocket watch. "The hour grows late, Marisa, and I must take my leave of you now."

Her eyes grew wide. "The hour is not so well advanced. I had thought you would stay a good deal later."

He got to his feet, seeming to be even taller in such a small room. "I have to attend a mill tomorrow which necessitates an early start."

"You are going out of Town?"

"Some distance. Then I intend to go on to one of my estates to consult with the land steward there. A visit is long overdue."

"Because of me?"

He smiled. "Yes, my dear, because of you."

Her countenance fell. "Then I shall not see you tomorrow?"

He looked down on her. "I'm afraid not. Shall you miss me?"

"It will be unbearable."

"Nuncton and Harwood will be only too pleased to bear you company in my stead."

"Do not tease me. I am devastated to see you go. When shall I see you again?"

"I shall send round a note the moment I return."

She gazed at him in astonishment and then smiled. "I shall miss you so much, *caro*."

He kissed her gently. "And I you."

She followed him towards the door. "Mayhap by the time I see you again our future together will be resolved."

"It is entirely possible."

He waved to her before he climbed into the carriage. The curtains were drawn and he sank back into the squabs, feeling unusually weary, although the day had not been busier than any other.

"To White's, my lord?" the driver enquired.

"No, take me home," he replied, much to the man's surprise.

The marquis closed his eyes as the carriage set off on its journey towards Piccadilly and he didn't open them again until he arrived. Candles were still alight in many windows of the house, he noted when he looked up at it. He hesitated for a long moment by the carriage before going inside.

As he handed his cloak to a rather sleepy footman, he asked, "Has Lady Emberay retired yet?"

"No, my lord. Lieutenant Peterson is still taking supper with her ladyship." The marquis stared at the man who then asked, "Shall I inform her ladyship that you are here, my lord?"

The marquis continued to stare at him for a long moment before he shook his head. "Don't disturb them. Goodnight."

"Goodnight, my lord," the lackey responded, watching him curiously as he walked with uncharacteristic slowness up the stairs. A moment later the fellow shrugged and went to snooze once again in an alcove.

Some time later, when Eliza came up to her room, she could hear movements in the adjoining room. She frowned for a moment as Dorcas brought her nightgown.

"It is rather late for my husband's valet to be at work, Dorcas. I wonder what he can be doing at this hour."

"It is not just Marlow in there, my lady. His lordship came home some considerable time ago."

Eliza stared at her maid in astonishment. "How odd. I was so certain Signora Tarrazi would have detained him for much longer than this."

The maidservant bit her lip. "If I may be permitted to say so, my lady, perchance his lordship is growing weary of her. It's bound to happen sooner or later."

"If only that were so, Dorcas," the marchioness murmured, "but I cannot credit it is. My husband would not easily fall under her spell, so it is like he will not weary of her soon."

"It might be that she grows weary of *him*. Signora Tarrazi—as she likes to be known—might well have had her head turned by all the attention she's been getting of late."

"She couldn't be such a buffle-head, although I own, if that occurred he might be devastated for a while but it would be better than what I am obliged to endure at present. My husband wouldn't wear the willow for long in any event."

The maid turned back the covers on the half-tester bed and removed the hot brick which was warming it. Eliza was still thoughtful as she climbed in, scarcely noticing Dorcas smoothing back the covers.

"Do you require anything more tonight, my lady?"

''No, Dorcas, I thank you. You may retire now.''

Eliza watched her maid extinguish all the remaining candles, and then, bobbing a curtsey, leave the room. She carried with her the last lighted candle, and immediately the room grew darker, lit now only by the dying embers of the fire. The house was quiet. At night the sound of scurrying feet of countless servants was silenced to be replaced by the creaking of floorboards and old timbers.

Someone was still moving about in the adjoining room, and Eliza could hear the dull buzz of conversation. Her heart ached despite the diverting company of Lieutenant Peterson who tried so hard to amuse her, and usually succeeded, but it was alone in the huge bed each night when her loneliness and heartache became acute. On so many evenings of late she had been obliged to lie wakeful and troubled, her mind filled with images of Marisa Tarrazi clutched in the marquis's arms.

After a while she turned on her side and closed her eyes, even though she knew she would not fall asleep so easily. Suddenly, however, she stiffened when there came a gentle knock on the communicating door.

A moment later it opened to admit a shaft of light. Eliza's heart beat unevenly as footsteps crossed the room which was lightened by the solitary candle the marquis was carrying. She kept her eyes closed and remained motionless in the bed as he came to stand in front of her. She felt his presence close to her and could reach out and touch him with very little effort. She sensed he was looking down at her, and he seemed to be there for an age. At last he moved away again, and after the door had closed behind him, Eliza moved to brush away the tears which had been squeezing from beneath her closed eyelids, and she stared up at the intricate pattern woven into the half-tester for a long time afterwards.

ELEVEN

"You must apprise me of your progress in this very delicate situation," Lady Bramwell told Eliza several days later as she breezed into her drawing-room.

The marchioness had been picking at the harpsichord in a desultory way, only the melancholy tunes had not diverted her mind at all. At least Rosamund Bramwell's visit might give her a little cheer, she reasoned.

"There has been none," Eliza replied, looking despondent. "Nothing has changed." At the sight of her friend's surprise Eliza quickly invited, "Oh, do be seated, Rosa dear. I am quite cork-brained these days."

Lady Bramwell seated herself in a bergère chair, facing her friend, and carefully removed her gloves. "I cannot conceive how that can be. Denzil has been seen *everywhere* in your company. Everyone remarks upon it, and I take leave to doubt that fact has escaped Emberay's notice."

"Naturally, he is fully aware of Lieutenant Peterson's presence at my side, but it seems to escape your notice that Emberay might simply not care what I do or with whom."

"I cannot credit him with such stupidity." Rosamund Bramwell gazed worriedly at her friend who appeared to be pale and listless. "If only you and Denzil really were—"

Eliza's eyes widened. "I fail to understand how that would help."

The countess laughed. "It would be so much better if you didn't care a jot what your husband did, or with whom."

"How I wish that were so too, Rosa, but I do care, so very much."

Lady Bramwell's eyes narrowed. "Eliza, has anything further transpired?"

"Nothing of any note—only—I am beginning to think it is worse than I feared."

"How can that possibly be? What can be worse than you being pained by Emberay's infatuation for this creature?"

Eliza laced her fingers together. "It is beginning to appear that he might wish to marry her."

Lady Bramwell was immediately taken aback. "Faddle! I am prepared to own that Emberay has suffered a temporary lunacy over this creature, but I cannot truly believe his attic is entirely to let!"

"If what I suspect is true, it is entirely possible I shall lose everything!"

"You have lost nothing as yet. He might well have some fleeting fever for her—while her popularity as a singer remains at a peak—but it will not last, nor shall his infatuation. I vow to you it will not. My dear Eliza, you have gained so many admirers of late. By comparison to that baggage you are a great beauty with the added bonus of being a lady of quality."

Eliza laughed harshly. "What moonshine."

"It is true, and it has always been so, only you haven't felt the need to be so flamboyant before."

"If it is as you say, it certainly does not weigh with

Emberay. Four-score gentlemen might find me entrancing, but it is nothing to me if he does not."

"You are being very provoking, Eliza. You seem to forget your situation is similar to that endured by most of us at some time or other. Just recall Bramwell and Elsa Fortesque only last Season."

"Forgive me for saying so, Rosa, but you are accustomed to such behaviour from Bramwell."

"Then you are more fortunate than you know that this has not occurred before."

Far from being comforted, Lady Emberay seemed more distressed than ever. "How I feel for poor Princess Caroline. She has been cast out, separated from her child and replaced by another woman. If the future King can behave in such a manner, what hope is there for anyone else?"

Lady Bramwell smiled. "My dear, Emberay is not in the least like the Prince of Wales. Your husband is no heartless boor. Oh dear, I pray you do not repeat that; I am persuaded it may be treason."

Eliza allowed herself a smile, and her friend smiled too. "That is so much better, Eliza. Do keep smiling whatever the provocation. Gentlemen like it, you know. There is nothing so off-putting as a Friday-face." After a pause she went on thoughtfully, "I have been quite persuaded that Emberay has been at home more often of late, and is seen in your company more frequently than is usual for him."

"He has been away for several days, to attend a mill and then some estate business."

"One thing is certain, she has not been with him. She was seen leaving the opera house in Dorrington's carriage last night. Emberay is certain to hear of it the moment he returns to Town. There will be a score of his cronies only too delighted to acquaint him with the information."

Eliza got up and walked to the window. "It is so unjust. There are so many men for her, Rosa, and only the one for me."

103

"You will win his heart yet, I vow. You have always dealt amicably together. He will not wish to change that for life with a virago—which I am assured she is."

Eliza turned to her and smiled. "The problem is that she will not act the virago in his sight."

Lady Bramwell hesitated a moment before venturing, "I think you should know there is an *on-dit* abroad regarding Signora Tarrazi's origins."

Eliza frowned. "Does it contain an element of the truth, Rosa?"

"Oh yes, indeed."

"Then how on earth—"

Her friend shrugged. "I have not mentioned a word of it to anyone, and I'll wager that my cousin has not, but you know how these rumours begin. She has deliberately cultivated a mystery about her origins, and now people are beginning to speculate for themselves. It is always so, and on this occasion what would normally be a malicious piece of tattle just happens to be the truth. I cannot understand your concern, Eliza. You seem intent upon protecting that baggage, which is exceeding crack-brained of you."

Eliza went back to the sofa and sat down again, clasping her hands tensely in front of her. "I know Emberay, you see. I understand him so well, and if I told him this news and hoped to alienate him from Signora Tarrazi, it would merely have the opposite effect. It would merely cause him to feel chivalrous towards her and want to protect her. I can only hope now that he will tire of her in time, although even if that happens before long there will be someone else to replace her in his affections. There always has been."

The countess drew a deep and heartfelt sigh. "You really are suffering the megrims, my dear. How odd Emberay's absence should do this to you. I positively welcome Bramwell's absence from Town."

This statement caused her friend to smile. "I cannot credit that, Rosa."

"We can gain nothing by discussing my marriage, which I find entirely satisfactory. Now tell me, Eliza, do you no longer wish to fight for his affections?"

After being taken aback for a few seconds the marchioness straightened up. "I most certainly do! I shall never give up."

Rosamund Bramwell smiled. "That is what I wished to hear. To be honest, my dear, when I see you in such determined heart, I fear for Signora Tarrazi."

Eliza laughed harshly. "I should not, Rosa, for I am persuaded my husband is in her company at this very moment, and loving every moment of it."

The Marquis of Emberay walked slowly through the rooms of White's Club. He nodded to several acquaintances and paused long enough to refuse to join a rubber of whist. He had about him the air of a man not quite decided what he should do. After exchanging greetings with Lord Alvaney, the marquis sat down in one of the deep leather chairs and picked up a copy of *The Morning Post*.

He had only just opened it when someone sat down in the chair next to his. Lord Emberay glanced around and was not well pleased to see Sir Hugo Nuncton.

"Good day to you, Emberay," the man greeted him brightly. "I notice you picked up the blunt on that black filly. It was a shrewd wager."

"Thank you, Nuncton," the marquis responded with rather less enthusiasm. "Am I to assume you lost?"

The other man smiled regretfully. "Alas it is so. My pockets are to let and I'm reduced to breaking shins. I don't suppose you—"

The marquis smiled, also with apparent regret. "Afraid not, Nuncton. My own finances are not too great. I have been obliged to pay some hefty bills of late."

105

"Indeed. I recall you have heavy commitments."

The marquis looked amused. "I am glad to see you recovered from our last encounter."

"We shall have to arrange a return bout. I vow you shall not win so easily next time."

"Whenever you wish."

The marquis was about to return his attention to his newspaper when Sir Hugo ventured, "It is rumoured you've been neglecting our little songbird of late."

"Since when has common gossip borne any relation to the truth?"

"Since Demsey and Wilcock have been seen with a certain lady on more than one occasion."

The marquis appeared to be vexed but replied in a careless tone, "I have been out of Town on business, although I have no doubt you and many others have prevented Signora Tarrazi—if that is to whom you refer—from feeling lonely in my absence."

"Oh, indeed, you may rely upon it, Emberay. I find it exceedingly pleasant to buy her a posy or a geegaw now and again. It is nothing too serious, you understand."

The marquis smiled deprecatingly. "You have always been considered a dilettante, Nuncton."

Not at all put out, the other man went on. "An hour or two with a fetching chit serves to take my mind off that bracket-faced baggage awaiting me at home, more often than not with a set-down."

"You cannot expect to elicit my pity," the marquis responded, his voice heavy with irony.

"I don't pity myself overmuch," Sir Hugo confessed, "although if I had a wife as fetching as Lady Emberay I wouldn't be so anxious to stay away from home." The marquis cast him a cold look, and Sir Hugo went on, apparently unaware of it, "Fetching chit, Lady Emberay. What a pity that Peterson fellow won't let anyone else near to her."

The marquis threw the newspaper down on a table. "I am certain your appreciation of my wife's attributes are very flattering, Nuncton, but before you address it to her, let me inform you she is a woman who does not believe in moonshine."

"Where your wife is concerned it is nought but the truth, and she is bound to know it. I am not the only man who thinks so. Moreover, I have yet to meet a female who wouldn't be in high snuff to be told she is beautiful." He sighed. "Females can be the devil, can they not, Emberay?"

"I am in agreement with you upon that observation, Nuncton," the other man replied in heartfelt tones.

He was about to get up when Sir Hugo mused, "Strange, the exotic foreign names some creatures feel bound to take on for themselves when they wish to become actresses or singers."

The marquis looked at him. "Is that a general remark, Nuncton, or do you refer to anyone in particular?"

"I don't suppose we should find exotic creatures quite so entrancing if they were called by more mundane names. One cannot blame these ladies. After all, Emberay, you will agree that a mysterious and romantic background is far more interesting."

The marquis continued to eye him coldly for a moment or two and then he did get to his feet. Nodding curtly he took his leave of the other man and went to seek out Foster Cullington, a friend of long standing.

The young man was, however, more than a little reluctant to leave his game of piquet, but at the marquis's insistence did so.

"Why are you in such a pucker, Emberay?" Mr. Cullington demanded as the marquis drew him into a corner.

"You were losing heavily and therefore should be grateful to me." He lowered his voice then to ask in a harsh whisper, "Is there some tattle about Town regarding Marisa?"

Mr. Cullington looked uncomfortable, but he laughed. "When is there not? Everyone adores speculating about her. She thrives on tattle."

"You did not answer my question, Cullington. Is there anything in particular being said about her origins?"

Mr. Cullington sighed. "It was only a matter of time before the matter reached your hearing. Town has been agog for the last few days. No one has spoken of anything else."

"I have been out of Town."

"So I understand." The other man's eyes narrowed. "You and La Tarrazi haven't parted company, have you? There has been a good deal of speculation."

"No. There was urgent business which needed attention, and a mill at Claverton." He smiled. "I wagered a pony on the winner." Then he frowned. "I needed time to think, Cullington. Matters, I confess, are moving far too briskly for my liking."

The other man looked concerned. "You're in this deep, are you not?"

"It is nothing from which I cannot extricate myself, but I should like to know just what is being said about Marisa."

"What have you already heard?"

"Apart from the fact she has been exceeding busy while I was out of Town, nothing very specific, only Nuncton just hurled a few heavy insinuations in my direction, which, added to several others I have heard, make me curious. Of course all those who have spoken to me have also pursued Marisa persistently to no avail. Naturally they feel bitter, although I confess to a certain curiosity. Not only that but Nuncton fancies my wife, the impudent puppy."

Foster Cullington laughed. "Lady Emberay has certainly become a high flyer of late. Maldon wagered Disworth a pony that Lady Emberay would take off with Peterson within the month.''

Fury filled the marquis's eyes and entire being although he contrived to remain outwardly calm. ''Did he indeed? He is certain to lose his purse.''

''Oh I do not doubt it,'' the other man replied, looking uncomfortable.

''Well, you have yet to tell me what is being said,'' the marquis demanded.

'' 'Tis merely tattle, Emberay. I'm persuaded there is no truth in it.''

The marquis gripped his friend's sleeve tightly. ''No truth in *what*?''

Foster Cullington extricated his sleeve and smoothed down the cloth. ''It is rumoured that La Tarrazi is actually from the East End and not Ravello. Naturally, if that is true it is also possible she has no Italian aristocratic connections either.''

''Have you any notion how the rumour began?''

''There is a seamstress who makes gowns for several ladies of the *ton*, who recognised her and was glad enough to acquaint her clients with the information.''

The marquis nodded. ''Thank you, Cullington. I am much obliged to you.''

As he turned on his heel Mr. Cullington asked in alarm, ''Where are you going?''

The marquis glanced back, his face impassive. ''Home, Cullington. I am going home.''

TWELVE

Every box was taken at the fashionable haunt of Vauxhall Gardens that evening. Present were a great many of Eliza's acquaintances, and she had dressed carefully in one of her new fashionable gowns, and had chosen her jewellery with care.

When the music began gentlemen flocked to the Bramwell's box in the hope that Eliza would stand up with them, and after a while she realised she truly did enjoy the attention she was receiving. It was a balm to her bruised pride, for everyone present also knew of the marquis's infatuation for La Tarrazi.

She had just returned to join her friends in the box after dancing the minuet with Lieutenant Peterson when the marquis arrived quite unexpectedly. Eliza stared at him in astonishment as he bade the others a good evening. Then he smiled at his wife, although she noted that his eyes remained cold.

"You look lovely this evening, my dear."

Flustered, and aware of the scrutiny of all the others, she replied, "Thank you," averted her eyes, and went to sit by Lieutenant Peterson who whispered, "How odd this is. He was at White's this afternoon and at Vauxhall tonight. I wonder when he finds time for La Tarrazi nowadays."

Eliza's cheeks were flushed with pleasure, and now she looked sharply at her companion before her attention was diverted towards the others once again.

"We do not usually look to see you at Vauxhall," Rosamund Bramwell ventured, viewing him through a quizzing-glass.

"You always find it so tedious," Mrs. Berriman added, swishing her fan to and fro. "Of course it is a very special evening," Phillida went on before he could reply. "Tonight we are fortunate that La Tarrazi is to sing for us."

The marquis's face became rather stiff. "I had no notion of that, but it will be an added pleasure."

All the pleasure the sight of him had aroused in Eliza vanished now. She understood his real reason for being there and she was furious with him. Her eyes flashed with anger which he affected not to notice, although she was certain he must have been aware of it.

The marquis glanced at her, saying, "Eliza, will you stand up with me for the cotillion?"

"How kind of you to ask, but I have promised the dance to Lieutenant Peterson," she replied, her voice tight with anger.

He smiled then, his charm very evident. It was an effort to Eliza to withstand it. "With your permission, Lieutenant Peterson. I am persuaded you will be willing to forgo the pleasure of standing up with my wife on this occasion. After all, you have already been privileged to dance with her this evening."

The young officer looked annoyed, but had no choice but to nod his assent. "And you, Lord Emberay, very rarely have the opportunity to stand up with your wife," he couldn't resist replying.

If the marquis was aware of the sarcasm, he did not acknowledge it. He merely held out his hand, and Eliza had no option but to take it. As they moved towards the dancers she spoke not a word to him.

When the music began she could not help but retort, "Wherever I go nowadays I seem to encounter Signora Tarrazi."

The marquis seemed not at all put out. "How odd you should say so, Eliza, for I was thinking precisely that of Lieutenant Peterson."

"He may be seen wherever he wishes with no harm done, but in Signora Tarrazi's instance she is so often in the public eye and I am very much afraid if she persists in singing on every possible occasion her audience is like to grow weary." The marquis appeared to be attending her raptly, and she added in a tart voice, "However, I have no doubt another Italian songbird will take her place, although I take leave to doubt that will be of any consolation to Signora Tarrazi."

When she had finished he asked politely, "Tell me, Eliza, does Lieutenant Peterson ever intend to return to his ship?"

"It is possible he will not."

The marquis looked surprised. "Evidently he finds the attractions of Town much more to his liking."

"I dare say. In any event he has made mention of resigning his commission, although I am not altogether certain the decision has actually been made."

"No doubt Lieutenant Peterson fancies himself as a man about Town."

"You sound a trifle disapproving, Max," Eliza responded, casting him a cool look.

"Oh, I assure you that isn't so, my dear. If Lieutenant Peterson amuses you I could not be more pleased for him to remain in Town."

"He does amuse me, although becoming a man about Town is not to my mind his true vocation."

"Indeed?"

He looked interested, and becoming slightly vexed Eliza told him, "I rather believe he would like a home and family."

One of the marquis's dark eyebrows rose a little. "You are exceeding well-acquainted with his wishes, Eliza. Has he also been kind enough to confide in you his choice of bride?"

"No," she replied irritably, and was glad to be parted from him temporarily.

When they met again the conversation was not resumed, much to her relief. The dance ended at last, and as the marquis escorted her from the dance floor they came almost face to face with Marisa Tarrazi who had strolled into the Pavilion. She looked incredibly lovely, dressed in pale blue muslin, a confection of blue feathers in her hair. She was escorted by a number of her admirers, including Sir Hugo Nuncton.

The singer was momentarily taken aback, but then she closed her fan with a decided snap, smiled and curtseyed low. "My lord, my lady." Her eyes narrowed suddenly as she straightened up. "This is both a surprise and a pleasure."

Eliza had recovered her dismay, and aware the meeting was being quizzed from all sides, smiled broadly and remained close to her husband's side.

"Hearing you sing is the prime reason for our presence here tonight," Eliza told her. "Vauxhall Gardens has never been so full for an age."

The woman eyed the marquis warily. "I hope you both will enjoy my singing."

"That is a foregone conclusion," the marquis told her. "Only the totally deaf could not."

Marisa Tarrazi looked gratified and yet not at ease. Sets were being made up for a country dance, and Sir Hugo stepped forward saying gallantly, "Is it possible I have at last an opportunity to stand up with you, Lady Emberay?

113

Your programme is usually filled at the outset of the evening.''

Eliza hesitated as she always did with Sir Hugo, but then she inclined her head, even though she doubted the wisdom of leaving her husband in the company of that woman. Her other escorts had drifted away when they became engaged in conversation.

"It will be a pleasure, Sir Hugo."

"Let us not argue upon whose pleasure is the greatest," he answered, and she smiled, a little wistfully.

The marquis bowed abruptly to them both and watched them take their place in the set. Eliza glanced across to where she had left them to see the marquis and Marisa Tarrazi walking slowly towards one of the dark walks, a sight which sent her spirits plunging.

When the music began she said to Sir Hugo, "You are a great admirer of Signora Tarrazi, are you not?"

"Are not we all, Lady Emberay?" he responded as they began to dance. A moment later he ventured, "Your husband, it appears, is still rather besotted by the Italian wench."

For a moment Eliza stiffened, and then she laughed. "Is she truly Italian, sir? In truth I have heard stories which countermand that theory."

"It really doesn't matter, my dear, for she is still able to surround herself with any number of admirers. However, you must know you could just as easily emulate her example. I, for one, would be foremost among your admirers."

Again Eliza was taken aback, and once more she laughed gaily despite wondering just where her husband was at that moment. "La, Sir Hugo, you would be obliged to be in two places at once."

"I think not, my lady, for I assure you I am in earnest."

His apparent sincerity, coupled with her intrinsic dislike of the man, contrived to make her feel uneasy. Oh, she loved the effect of her flirting—it was a totally new power—but it was still true she wanted only one man to respond to it.

However, she cast Sir Hugo a coy look and replied, "You may be certain I shall bear what you say in the forefront of my mind."

The air beyond the Pavilion was cool and sharp. Marisa Tarrazi glanced at the marquis as they walked away from the noise and the crowds, saying a mite reproachfully, "How ill-used I am, Lord Emberay. I haven't clapped eyes upon you in an age and I certainly had no notion you were back in Town."

"Fortunately you were not lonely in my absence."

She wagged her fan at him. "Do I detect a note of jealousy, *caro*?"

He eyed her dispassionately. "Do you, Marisa? You must decide for yourself."

She cast him a speculative look before saying softly, "*Caro*, I cannot stop gentlemen admiring me, but I do not have to reciprocate the feeling. I can love only one man, and I have been utterly desolate in his absence."

"Did you love your husband too, Marisa?"

Several shadowy figures flitted past, some laughing, others embracing in the shadows where light from the Chinese lanterns did not penetrate.

"Yes, oh yes, I did," she answered, pausing to look up at him. "He was a fine man and so well-connected. I was devastated for a long time after we were parted so soon after our marriage."

"How did he die? I don't believe you ever told me that."

"It was a putrid fever," she answered sadly. "I watched him die and could do nothing to save him. My agony was as great as his." Marisa Tarrazi looked up into the marquis's eyes and smiled. "But I am the most fortunate creature alive. I am in love again with a wonderful gentleman.

115

Tell me, *cara*, did you contrive to speak with Lady Emberay?''

"About what?''

A look of vexation flitted across her features, but she continued to smile. "About us, *caro*.''

"The opportunity has not arisen.''

"Lady Emberay is still very much engaged by the handsome Lieutenant Peterson, but on a matter of this import you really must find time to speak with her.''

He sighed profoundly. "Yes, I must.''

She appeared satisfied then. "And although I am reluctant to part from you so soon I must prepare for my performance.''

"Of course,'' he answered stiffly.

She looked at him curiously. "Are you quite certain I have done nothing to anger you, *caro*?''

By way of a reply he drew her close and kissed her roughly. Laughing, she drew away, saying, "You have missed me. I am certain of it now.'' She straightened the feathers in her hair. "I will sing so much better tonight knowing you are in the audience.'' He was looking down at her, and she kissed his lips lightly. "Will you come to me after the performance, *caro*?''

"I have already been obliged to accept an invitation.''

Once again she looked vexed. "Can you not cry off?''

He seemed regretful. "Not on this occasion.''

"Then when shall I be honoured by a visit from you?''

"I shall call on you tomorrow, if I may.''

Marisa Tarrazi opened her fan as he escorted her back towards the Pavilion. "That is something I shall await with great impatience.''

Eliza was already ensconced in the Bramwell's box when her husband joined them for supper. There was no telling look upon his face, but she had always found him inscrutible at times.

Phillida Berriman eyed him with amusement as she

forked some ham into her mouth. "La! You are exceeding tardy, Lord Emberay. We have all but finished supper. There is very little left."

The marquis cast her an ironic smile. "There is more than enough for me, Mrs. Berriman, but perchance you would wish me to order more for you."

She didn't trouble to reply to his sarcasm as he eyed her full plate but commented, "I trust whatever detained you was of great import to delay your supper."

"It was, Mrs. Berriman," he answered shortly.

"I cannot wait to hear Signora Tarrazi sing," she prattled on. "Do you think it true," she asked of no one in particular, "that the nearest she has been to Italy is the West India docks?"

The marquis had helped himself to a small portion of food, but then he looked at the woman coldly. Most people would have been chilled into silence by such a look, but Phillida Berriman was not one of their number.

Lady Bramwell glanced at Eliza apologetically before saying in a firm voice, "I have it on very good authority that it is absolutely true."

"What do *you* think, Lord Emberay?" Mrs. Berriman asked artlessly, pointing her fork in his direction. "After all, your acquaintance with La Tarrazi is much greater than ours."

The marquis had begun to eat his supper. Eliza glanced at her husband worriedly as he replied with no apparent concern, "I think she is an exceeding good singer, Mrs. Berriman."

"But what of her origins?" the woman persisted. "Do you not find the speculation fascinating? I confess that I do. I was never taken in by her as so many others evidently were."

The marquis was beginning to look more than a little vexed. Eliza was watching him anxiously. "Does it matter?" she asked. "All which really matters is her ability

117

to entertain us, which she does quite splendidly. Her origins are of no import whatsoever."

The marquis cast her an admiring glance, but not to be outdone, Phillida Berriman added, "Oh, I am persuaded she certainly must excel at entertaining."

"And from all I have heard at quite a rate of knots," Lieutenant Peterson added, causing the group to laugh.

The marquis did not join in the laughter. His colour seemed to deepen and his eyes burned darkly. Eliza glanced at him worriedly again, and she longed to go to him, but as Marisa Tarrazi was introduced to the audience she sat back in her chair and prepared to applaud and enthuse over a woman she had come to loathe and fear.

THIRTEEN

It came as a great surprise to Eliza to find her husband taking breakfast the following morning. When she went into the breakfast-room he paused to smile at her.

"Good morning, Eliza. Did you sleep well?"

"My sleep, as always, was undisturbed," she replied with heavy irony, recovering from her initial surprise.

After a few moments she went to sit at the table, facing him. A footman brought fresh coffee and toast, and the marquis said, "Do have some eggs, Eliza. They really are very good."

She accepted some onto her plate while eyeing him covertly. He really did look splendid in his brown riding-coat. She wondered why he was in such good spirits, and supposed Marisa Tarrazi's triumph at Vauxhall was the reason for him being in such high snuff that morning.

"There is a letter for you," he told her, a few moments later. "I recognise Horatia's hand."

Eliza accepted it from him in silence and broke the seal, quickly scanning the page. As she did so the marquis ventured, "Horatia is in fine health and spirits, I trust."

"They are excellent," Eliza replied. "Horatia has enjoyed her stay with Dorinda and the children."

"I am delighted to hear that something has pleased her at last," he said wryly.

Eliza eyed him from over the page, "However, she does speak of returning to Town in the near future."

His face took on an expression of dismay. "Good grief! Not now of all times."

Eliza's look was one of mild surprise. "Why should she not return now?"

He appeared uncharacteristically discomposed. "All I meant was that she should remain in Devon for the present. The air is better for her than in Town. Wychcombe is better for her health and you must write immediately and tell her so."

Eliza folded the letter and smiled at him, hardly able to conceal her amusement. "You have the look of a guilty schoolboy, Max. She is your own sister and you are, remember, head of this family. Yet she invariably puts you in a pucker."

He was all at once abashed. "It's a matter of old habits, Eliza. When my mother died we were all very young. Horatia took over as a surrogate mother, being the eldest of us all, and she took her duties a mite seriously, I fear. That is why thoughts of Horatia invariably invoke guilt. In Horatia's opinion we were always guilty of some misdemeanour. In view of the kind of lifestyle my brother followed, my sister must believe she brought up a nest of cuckoos."

Eliza laughed, and it was almost as it used to be between them—almost but not quite. The difference was that Eliza no longer felt content, nor the old security. It was as if her home and family were under attack. Not only that; she also felt a constant yearning and a hunger she had not experienced before, and he, beneath the urbane exterior, was a troubled man. Eliza was in no doubt of that either.

"I can understand her dismay over your brother, but you have always led a blameless life, Max."

He glanced at her quickly and away again as she went

on, "At least I had no such problems with my creole nursemaid in Jamaica. I led a very carefree life."

"You were fortunate indeed," he agreed, "as are our children."

"They do have two parents which we did not have from a very early age."

"Quite so," he said quickly without looking at her, and then, "I did wonder if you intended to attend the balloon ascent today."

"I'm given to understand it is to be a spectacular event and I thought I would take Kit and Lucy to see it."

He gave her a searching look. "And Lieutenant Peterson?"

Eliza affected a nonchalant air. "I have no notion what he is doing today."

The marquis drew in a quick breath. "Mayhap Kit would like to ride with me in the phaeton. You could take Lucy and her nursemaid in the barouche and meet us there."

Eliza's eyes glowed with warmth and pleasure. "What an excellent notion. Kit will love to ride with you. It will give him a good deal of pleasure."

"No more than I, but it had occurred to me," he went on, again without looking at her, "that we have not enjoyed being together as a family for a while."

Eliza had been affecting great unconcern, but now she stopped eating and looked at him. "We both have heavy social engagements during the Season, but we do get together as a family when we are at Brockway in the summer." She hesitated before asking, almost fearfully, "You do intend us to go there this year, do you not?"

"Oh yes, yes indeed," he answered vaguely, leaving Eliza more worried than before.

Suddenly she had a vision of being banished to some villa in Kensington while Marisa Tarrazi took over the house and the children, allowing Eliza access only on rare occasions, if at all. Everyone knew of Princess Caroline's desperate attempts to see her own daughter, the future Queen, to no avail. Eliza's fingers tightened over her fork, for she knew she would die if that happened to her.

Unaware of his wife's fears the marquis dabbed at his lips with his napkin and then pushed back his chair. "I shall see you later in the Park, my dear, but mayhap you would instruct the nursemaid to have Kit ready in his outdoor clothes."

"Yes, I will certainly do so," she replied, still preoccupied by her disturbing thoughts. She watched him go and then, drawing a sigh, began to read through some of the cards which had been left the day before.

When Eliza arrived at Hyde Park in the barouche a great many other carriages were already there to watch the spectacle of a hot-air balloon making an ascent over London. The driver was obliged to make several circuits of the area before Lord Emberay's phaeton could be located. At last it was seen, and when the barouche came to a halt the marquis hurried to help Eliza down.

She had taken great pains in choosing her clothes and bonnet, and it gratified her to see the admiration in his eyes as he handed her down. He held onto her hand for a long moment before drawing her closer.

"Eliza," he said softly.

The look on his face caused her heart to flutter unevenly and her mouth to go dry. Then a passing buck pushed past and the marquis let her hand go. He turned to take Lucy from her nursemaid while Eliza watched him longingly. As he put the child down on the ground Kit came racing up to them. The spell was broken, but Eliza felt there was a closeness between them which had been missing for a long time.

"Mama, we have just seen a tumbler doing the most amazing feats," Kit told her excitedly.

"You must show me where he is, dearest," she replied,

still a little breathless. She glanced at her husband who was gazing at her, and she knew her cheeks had grown pink.

They began to walk in the direction of the balloon which was being inflated at a steady rate. The area was crowded with spectators, and hawkers anxious to ply their wares. People of all classes mixed easily for once.

A gypsy pushed a bunch of heather in front of Eliza's face, causing her to draw back. "Bring you good fortune, lady. Buy my heather."

Eliza glanced at her husband. "Do I need heather to bring me good fortune, Max?"

He smiled faintly and tossed the woman a coin. "We all need a little assistance some time, Eliza."

Clutching the heather they moved on, Kit saying, "Hurry, Mama. Oh do hurry."

"Lucy isn't able to walk as fast as you," Eliza scolded, "so we cannot go any quicker."

"Cannot Anna carry her?"

"We are almost there now. Did you arrive a long time before we did?"

"Quite a while."

"Due to Kit, let me say," the marquis informed her.

She looked amused. "I cannot conceive how."

"Papa allowed me to tool the ribbons on our way here," the boy confided, and Eliza felt faint at the thought.

A moment later she cast her husband a reproachful look. "Oh, Max, you didn't."

"He has to learn at some time."

"But he is far too young!"

"I held them, you chuckle-head," he whispered, "but don't let Kit know."

She smiled with relief as another gypsy offered, "Let me read yer palm, m'lady. Let me tell you what life's got in store."

The marquis looked at his wife enquiringly, but she

shook her head. The last thing she wanted was to know her future. Just then it didn't bear too close a scrutiny.

Nearer to the balloon itself a tumbler was making a display of great agility. It gave Eliza much satisfaction to see her son's pleasure, and she was more than a little pleased that those who found the Tarrazi affair so diverting would see them abroad as an apparently happy family. If only, she thought, she could rid herself of the notion the marquis was preparing her gently for the crushing blow to follow. His sudden solicitude bore all the hallmarks of that.

The tumbler finished his act to great applause. The marquis lifted Lucy up so she could see better when a juggler began to perform his tricks. Watching them, Eliza realised she hadn't felt so happy in a long time, and it was merely her husband's presence which gave her so much pleasure, for her worries were certainly no less. Suddenly aware of his scrutiny she smiled at him, and her heart lurched painfully when her eyes met his.

"Have you ever paused to consider, Eliza, how much you and I have changed since we first met?"

"I have never thought of it before, but we have, of course. You were obliged to become more responsible than ever before, and I grew up more quickly than I would otherwise have done."

"You were a child then; now you are a woman. You're not the same person and neither am I."

She looked away in distress, for his words struck dread in her heart. They seemed to bear an ominous ring.

A murmur of excitement passed around the crowd, for the balloonist was climbing into the basket at last. Kit was jumping up and down with excitement at the imminent departure of the balloon. A group of acquaintances descended upon the Emberays at that moment, and everyone chattered excitedly about the spectacle they had gathered there to witness.

"There are plans to re-enact the Battle of Trafalgar on the Serpentine," someone told her, and everyone agreed it was an exciting prospect.

"What a happy circumstance," Lieutenant Peterson declared as he joined the group a few minutes later. "I had not looked to see you here, my lady."

"But how opportune an encounter," Eliza cried, greeting him happily. "I have just been told it is planned to re-enact the Battle of Trafalgar on the Serpentine. You are eminently suited to advising on the event."

"There are those far more qualified than I," he responded, taking in the family group with one glance.

He nodded affably at Lord Emberay who cast him a cold look before turning away. Aware of the rapidly cooling atmosphere, Eliza said in a bright tone, "La! How exciting this is. It looks so dangerous. I trust that the gentleman will be safe in that contraption."

"There is certainly no guarantee of it, my lady," responded one of their acquaintances, "and I dare say that is what makes it so wonderful to observe."

"How goulish we must be," she responded with a shudder.

Casting another look at her husband she smiled uncertainly at Lieutenant Peterson who whispered as the balloon jerked against the ropes causing the crowd to gasp, "It warms my heart to see you here with Lord Emberay, my lady."

"I fear for what will come after it," she replied. "My husband is wont to make cryptic remarks of late."

"That is not necessarily a bad thing. He may be uncertain of you now, for you have gained so many admirers of late."

"I am most definitely uncertain of him, you may be sure. I sense that this matter is reaching a crisis point."

"That is my observation too, and mayhap it is time I faded from the scene for a short while."

She looked at him in alarm. "I cannot conceive how that will help."

"The object was to make Emberay aware of you as a woman and perchance jealous of my attention. If I always remain near you he cannot possibly declare his true feelings."

"I fear what they might be, but I do thank you for your concern and help, my dear Lieutenant Peterson. What you say is as always full of sense, and if I must face the fact that my marriage is to end I may as well do it now. I—we—have done all that is possible to avert the catastrophe."

"I am by no means certain you need be so despondent, my lady."

"Oh, how I pray you are correct, but I shall not cling to my husband if he loves another." She cast him a curious glance, attempting to push her own heartache to one side. "Do you intend to return to your ship?"

He straightened up, staring across the field. "I haven't yet decided, and in the meantime I wish to visit my sister who has been delivered of her first child."

"Then there is hope of seeing you in Town again before long?"

He smiled down at her. "Be assured I shall not rejoin my ship before taking my leave of you, my lady."

There was another loud gasp as the mooring-ropes were cut and the balloon slowly and unsteadily rose into the air. The gasps turned to cheers as the balloon quickly moved upwards, caught by gusts of the cool winter air.

"If you are in need of me, my lady," Lieutenant Peterson whispered, "Lady Bramwell will know where to reach me."

The balloon was drifting swiftly up into the sky, becoming smaller all the while. Eliza shaded her eyes to see it go. "There are times when I wish I could fly away in one of those contraptions," she sighed.

"Even Mr. Fletcher will be obliged to come down to earth again before long."

She smiled faintly, her demeanour one of all-pervading sadness in direct contrast to her more usual cheerful nature and the gaiety she had feigned of late to hide her unhappiness.

Kit came running up to them, flushed with excitement. "Did you ever see anything so remarkable, Lieutenant Peterson?"

"It was indeed amazing," the young man agreed.

"I would like to fly in a balloon," the child said breathlessly. "I would go right above the clouds."

"When you grow a little more you may do so," Lieutenant Peterson told him.

The marquis had been staring at them for a few minutes from a short distance away. As the crowd began to disperse, he approached, handing Lucy to her nursemaid who had been watching the proceedings and was still open-mouthed.

"Good day, Lord Emberay," the officer greeted him warmly, doffing his high-crowned beaver.

"We did not look to see you here today," the marquis replied, exhibiting no matching warmth of manner.

"I had not, in all truth, intended to come, and it was a last-minute decision. However, after witnessing the amazing spectacle I cannot regret it."

To Eliza's dismay she realised belatedly the marquis had once again become distant and withdrawn, looking at her as if she were a stranger.

"In that event," the marquis replied in clipped tones, "mayhap you will be good enough to escort Lady Emberay and our children home. I have an engagement to keep that will not wait."

"As you wish, my lord. It will be my privilege," Lieutenant Peterson replied, as astonished as Eliza.

The marquis tipped his hat and strode away towards his phaeton before Eliza could even say "Goodbye."

"I would be obtuse indeed if I imagined Lord Emberay was delighted to see me," the young man told her.

Watching the marquis's retreating figure his wife replied, "That is of no significance."

"He was in a mighty hurry to leave."

"He is going to her," she murmured.

"You cannot be certain," Lieutenant Peterson told her as gently as he could.

Eliza continued to watch her husband until he had been swallowed up in the crowds, and then looked at the young man. "I have learned to read the signs. When he becomes withdrawn it is because he feels a modicum of guilt."

"Did the change in his manner occur—after I had arrived?"

"Yes, I believe it did," she replied thoughtfully.

"Then I believe, more than ever, that it is as well I am leaving Town for a while."

She cast him a curious look, and it was at that moment Kit came running back to them. "Am I not going to drive Papa's phaeton on the way home, Mama?"

"We're going home in the barouche," Eliza answered, almost absently, trying desperately to hide her distress from the child.

"But I wanted to tool the ribbons again!"

"Another time," his mother assured him as they began to walk back towards the carriage, her fleeting pleasure dissipated entirely.

FOURTEEN

Marisa Tarrazi strode across the room and pulled furiously at the bell-rope. When her maid appeared she rounded on her furiously.

"Why did you not come to me immediately?" the singer demanded. "I have been obliged to ring for an unconscionable time."

"Signora, I came as quickly as I could. I thought Lord Emberay was still here."

Marisa Tarrazi put one hand to her head. "Never mind about that now."

"Signora, what is it you wish?"

"I must do something—something, only I don't know what."

The maid frowned. "Signora?"

"Something is amiss, Mimsie. I feel it in my bones. He vows eternal love, but he still has not spoken of a divorce to his wife."

"He might not wish to wound her."

"She is not so vapourish, mark my words. He underestimates that woman. She has a lover of her own and I am persuaded will welcome the break. In any event, theirs has always been an empty marriage, contracted for convenience only. A divorce can only benefit the both of them."

Marisa Tarrazi began to pace up and down, and the maid

gazed at her uncertainly. "Signora, what are you to do? His lordship might well shy away from the scandal involved."

"My lord Emberay shies away from nothing. He knows as well as I that the scandal will last not a sennight, or only until another takes its place." Again she put one hand to her head. "I have noticed of late he seems preoccupied with his thoughts whereas once he concerned himself only with me. Oh, I am weary of this life. I no longer wish to have to sing, to be amiable to old rakes and curtsey to their hag-ridden wives. I want an establishment of my own and a high position in Society, and I know this is my last opportunity to achieve my wish. I cannot let it go by."

"Signora, did you not tell me that Lord Emberay offered you an income and an establishment of your own?"

The woman's face twisted into a grimace. "It was a tempting offer, but this is my one chance to become a lady of quality. I must succeed, for I vowed it would come to pass a long time ago." She shook her head. "I grow so weary of being a basket-scrambler, obliged to grease the boots of those I despise. It is time those top-lofty lords and ladies toadied to *me*." She threw back her head, and her eyes were bright. Her maid almost felt afraid. "I am heartily tired of their condescension. Do you think I want to remain his lightskirt? What will happen when he tires of me? When I grow old and his fancy turns to a young chit? I am done with such uncertainties. No other admirer is so wealthy or has such an old title, and," she added with a sigh, "he is very much to my fancy."

Mimsie continued to stare at her helplessly, and then Marisa Tarrazi dashed across the room. "Fetch my pelisse and bonnet, and summon the carriage."

The maid looked startled despite being accustomed to her mistress's moods. "Which bonnet and pelisse do you require, signora?"

"Oh, does it matter? The brown. Yes, that will do, but be quick before my courage fails me."

The maid continued to stare at her in astonishment, and then Marisa Tarrazi's cheeks grew pink. "Well, what are you waiting for? Do as I tell you! There is work to be done to-day."

Mimsie gave her one last worried look before fleeing from the room, leaving Marisa Tarrazi to pace back and forth like a restless tiger in its cage at the zoo.

Lady Emberay was rocking her daughter on her knee in a rather desultory way. Her thoughts were still chaotic. It had been several days since Lieutenant Peterson had left Town, and she missed his company sorely. During that time she had seen very little of her husband, hardly at all since the balloon ascent. Naturally, Eliza had formed a shrewd suspicion about where he might be found.

At Eliza's feet her son played happily with his lead soldiers, although he displayed a rather ruthless streak when he knocked them down.

"I wonder if I may have some toy sailors," the child asked after a few moments, looking up at his mother hopefully. "And a wooden ship to put them in."

Eliza laughed in surprise. "I dare say it is possible, but why would you want any? You have always liked your soldiers and played with them for hours quite contentedly."

"The navy is far superior to the army in my opinion." He looked up at her with eyes remarkably like his father's. "Was Papa a hero when he was in the army?"

"All our soldiers and sailors are heroes, Kit, and your father was very brave."

"Do you think he's sorry he's not a soldier now?"

"I don't truly know that, dearest, but I'm persuaded he would still be in the army were it not for family commitments which were rather heavy."

"I wonder if he killed any Frenchies?" the boy murmured as he moved his soldiers around the imaginary battlefield.

"You really are blood-thirsty," Eliza told him indulgently.

Lucy squirmed off her mother's knee, knocking down most of her brother's soldiers in the process.

"Oh you stupid girl!" Kit cried, pushing her out of the way. "Girls are horrid, horrid, horrid!"

Lucy's lips began to curl at such harshness, and Eliza said quickly, "It was an accident, Kit. She didn't mean to knock your soldiers over."

"She has spoiled my game and I hate her!" the boy wailed.

Eliza quickly got up, glancing at the nursemaid who was attempting to comfort the whimpering Lucy. "I think you had better take them upstairs, Anna."

Frustrated at not being able to stand his soldiers up quickly enough the little boy burst into tears. "Now, now," Eliza scolded gently. "There is no cause to get into such a taking. Young men don't cry over such trifling matters. What would you do if you were an officer and those were your men? You wouldn't stand on the battlefield and cry, would you?"

He blinked back his tears bravely. "No, Mama. It was not that. I have the headache, I think."

His mother was immediately concerned and glanced once again at Anna. "He does look a trifle peaked."

"He's been fretful all day, my lady," the nursemaid confirmed.

"Mayhap you had better put him to bed with a hot brick and make a posset for him."

"Yes, my lady," the nursemaid replied, curtseying and gathering together the fretful children.

Eliza smiled to herself as they left the room, and then drew a sigh. She picked up her sewing, but no sooner had the door closed than it opened again, this time to admit the house-steward.

"What is it, Rainnes?" she asked, her attention only partially on the man.

"There is someone to see you, my lady," he announced, a mite disdainfully. He held out a silver salver, and Eliza took the card borne on it, glancing at it curiously.

She drew in a sharp breath as she read the name of Marisa Tarrazi. Countless thoughts flashed through her mind as she allowed the card to flutter back onto the tray. It was very tempting for Eliza to refuse to see this impudent woman, but after a moment her panic subsided and she looked at the house-steward.

"Show her up." As the servant turned away she added, "First of all send someone to clear away these toys, and I wish Arthur to show Signora Tarrazi up. No one else. Is that clear?"

The house-steward looked surprised, but replied, "As you wish, my lady."

Some minutes later Marisa Tarrazi was ushered into the immaculate drawing-room by the smirking footman. The singer looked ill at ease, and by comparison Eliza appeared totally relaxed.

"Signora Tarrazi," she greeted her. "What a pleasant surprise."

"I am honoured you condescended to see me, my lady."

Eliza ushered her to a seat, and the woman came across the room. Eliza smiled, "On the contrary, no one with an ounce of sensibility could turn away someone who has taken the Town by a storm."

The other woman smiled uncertainly, and Eliza went on, "Unfortunately I am only able to allow you a few minutes of my time as I have an engagement to fulfil this afternoon."

"You are a very busy lady."

"Yes, indeed, but may I procure for you some refreshment, Signora Tarrazi? A glass of ratafia, perchance."

"No, I thank you. I shall not detain you for long, my lady. While I was waiting to be shown up I could not help but admire your house. It is magnificent."

Eliza affected due gratification. "How kind of you to say so. Of course, our houses in England, however grand, cannot compare with those in Italy. You must know how inferior ours are by comparison. I can understand why so many of our English houses have been copied from their Italian counterparts. I know only from what my uncle has told me. He travelled extensively on a Grand Tour and visited many Italian cities. He is a learned man and I value his counsel.''

To Eliza's satisfaction the other woman continued to look ill at ease. ''Your ladyship is fortunate to have access to such counsel. I am totally alone in the world.''

''Tush. You have countless acquaintances—people who regard you very fondly indeed, my dear.''

''It is not quite the same, my lady.''

Eliza adjusted the folds of her skirt carefully before smiling kindly, ''Perhaps not.'' She glanced around the room. ''Speaking of houses, this place was, when I married Emberay, virtually derelict. Can you credit it now?''

The woman appeared vexed, no doubt at Eliza's meaningless chatter, which inclined her to continue. ''The curtains were mere tatters and the carpets threadbare. The furniture I scarce need to tell you was in an appalling condition. It took me all of three years to put it to rights.''

Marisa Tarrazi was evidently discomforted. ''It does you great credit, my lady. You have excellent taste.''

''Thank you, Signora Tarrazi. You are very gracious, but I have merely built on what was here already. You see, the Emberays are such an old family, dating back to King William the First. My husband's ancestors came over from Normandy to fight at King William's side and were afterwards rewarded with land and titles which somehow they have contrived to retain to this day. I own, signora, that the heritage is an awesome burden for someone as ordinary as I am.''

''You surely do yourself a grievous injustice, my lady.''

''So my husband is always telling me when I am derisory. You see, Signora Tarrazi, I can only trace my origins back to the reign of James the First.''

The woman's face grew dark as she replied, ''How provoking for you, my lady.''

Eliza laughed. ''My dear, how tedious this must all seem

to you, who comes from a country steeped in such glorious history. Tell me, signora, do you sing tonight?''

The woman looked in a small measure relieved that the question did not concern her own antecedents. ''No, my lady, not tonight.''

''That is a pity. I had hoped to visit the opera tonight, but no doubt we shall have the pleasure of hearing and seeing you perform on another occasion soon. The public will demand the opportunity.''

Marisa Tarrazi glanced around the gracious room before looking at the marchioness once again. ''I suppose you already know that the footman who showed me up here is an old acquaintance of mine.''

Eliza frowned. ''Really? That must be Arthur to whom you refer, so I cannot conceive how that can be. An old acquaintance, did you say? As I understand it you have been in this country for only a short while, and Arthur has been in my service for several years.''

The woman drew in a sharp breath. ''You may have heard some rumour that I am not, in fact, Italian.''

Eliza shook her head. ''Indeed I have and, my dear, may I say what nonsense it is? You must not let it trouble your head. Whenever someone reaches your height of popularity and success tattle inevitably follows, and it is rarely of a complimentary nature. I invariably disregard tattle when it concerns someone I know and admire.''

''I am greatly relieved to hear you say so, my lady, but I would dearly like to know from whom the tattle originated.''

''I can well understand that, and if I discover the coxcomb I shall take great pleasure in informing you of his identity myself.''

The woman lowered her eyes. ''I am obliged to you, my lady.'' After a moment's pause she went on, ''I trust that Lord Emberay is in fine health and spirits.''

''Never more so,'' Eliza replied, with great enthusiasm. ''My husband, as I am sure you must know, signora, enjoys all aspects of life to the full. Ah, if only I possessed just a small amount of his zest for pleasure. I dare say it is child-bearing which makes females less able to enjoy the freedom to indulge in endless frolics. Do you—have any offspring, Signora Tarrazi? I have two.''

''My husband died only a short while after our marriage.''

Eliza appeared to be devastated. ''How tragic. I'm so pleased that life is treating you more kindly these days.''

''Lord Emberay has helped divert me of late.''

Eliza smiled with pleasure which discomposed the other woman even further. ''He would. He is always as gay as a goose in a gutter. I wish I could be as often in high snuff.''

Signora Tarrazi smiled then. ''Yes, I own, that is my opinion of him too. Such gentlemen are not rare, but how difficult it is for ladies to keep pace with them.''

''Oh, my dear Signora Tarrazi, I really wouldn't dream of trying.''

The other woman raised her eyes to meet Eliza's, and it was for the first time since she had entered the drawing-room. ''Lady Emberay, you are not a bufflehead, you must know that his lordship is in love with me and has been for some considerable time.''

Eliza's heart almost stopped, and then, as if to make up for the omission, began to beat twice as fast. She swallowed the lump that had formed in her throat and laughed. ''My dear Signora Tarrazi, of course he is! It is scarce a secret. He adores you and quite understandably too.''

Signora Tarrazi stared at Eliza wide-eyed. ''It does not trouble you that he is in love with me?''

''Not at all. It is not as if this were the first occasion my husband has been in love. My dear Signora Tarrazi, he is *always* in love. It is what makes him the fascinating man we both admire. Last Season he was in love with an opera dan-cer—Mary. No, Mary was not *her* name. I cannot think why that name comes so easily to mind.'' Eliza frowned with concentration. ''Marguerite. No it was not that either. Ah yes, I recall it now. *Martha*. Martha Dulaine. Declared herself a French emigrée, if you please. Such impudence, I declare. Once Emberay discovered she was not, his interest waned rather abruptly, and she was ravishingly beautiful. It was galling, I own. Before Martha Dulaine there were others, of course. I really have lost count of them, mainly because they were demi-reps and I wouldn't know them, of course. This time, with you, signora, he has displayed much improved taste.''

In the face of Eliza's light-heartedness the other woman looked vexed. ''Lady Emberay, I don't believe you appreciate the seriousness of this matter. Lord Emberay and I wish to marry.''

Eliza was wide-eyed. ''Signora Tarrazi, that is not possible for he is married to *me*.''

''That is easily remedied. I am persuaded you are not unaware your husband wishes to divorce you.''

It was as if this woman had thrust a knife into her heart, but Eliza was not so much hurt as angry now. She had the irrational urge to strike this presumptuous upstart, but somehow, despite her true feelings, contrived to continue to look amused.

''How famous! Did he tell you so?''

''We have discussed the matter on several occasions,'' Signora Tarrazi informed Eliza, exhibiting quiet dignity.

''I see,'' Eliza breathed.

''Do you, my lady?'' Marisa Tarrazi enquired.

Then Eliza sat back in the chair and eyed the woman with some amusement. ''Oh, my goodness. It really is very bad of him, signora. I had no notion he was still telling those Banbury Tales although I feared as much. He really is past praying for, I fear.''

The other woman looked bewildered by Eliza's reaction, and that, of course, was her intention. ''I do not quite understand, my lady.''

''I am certain you do not, and who can blame you? The

fact is, you must not believe my husband's moonshine, for he can lie faster than a dog can trot. It has always been so, and in mitigation I must say he means no harm by it. I am quite out of patience with him on this occasion, however. I would not have him fill *your* head with flummery, but he cannot help telling such Banbury Tales to any beautiful woman, and you are beautiful, my dear.''

Marisa Tarrazi sat forward. ''You are mistaken to take this so lightly, for he is deadly serious on this occasion, Lady Emberay.''

Eliza's smile faded. ''I take leave to doubt it.'' She gazed at the other woman pityingly, taking some consolation in her evident perplexity.

Marisa Tarrazi could sit still no longer. She jumped to her feet and began to move restlessly around. By comparison Eliza was remarkably calm and totally in control of herself. It was her only consolation.

''I thought you might welcome the notion,'' the woman said after a moment.

''I cannot conceive why. Emberay and I have a tolerable marriage I assure you. We rarely have occasion to disagree.''

Signora Tarrazi looked accusingly at the marchioness. ''You have a lover of your own.''

Eliza laughed. ''Oh, Lieutenant Peterson. Naturally, he is madly in love with me and in truth exceeding diverting, but he doesn't expect to marry me, no more than Emberay intends to become leg-shackled to you.'' Her eyes darkened momentarily with pain and anger. ''You have allowed yourself to believe the romantic fairy tales you sing about.''

The woman snatched up her reticule. ''It is you who are the fool, my lady. If your husband is constantly unfaithful, is it not because you fail to fulfil his needs?'' She drew in a deep breath. ''You need not suffer my presence any longer for I am persuaded Lord Emberay will be able to convince you of his true wishes, at which time you will be obliged to take note of them. Good day, *my lady*," she added with a sneer, sketching a curtsey.

As the door banged shut behind her, Eliza's composure, fragile enough at best, crumpled at last. Tears rolled down her cheeks and despair invaded her heart. After a few moments she stood up slowly and unsteadily, holding on to the back of the chair for support. Glancing out of the window she saw the marquis's phaeton pulling into the courtyard, something which sent her hurrying to the bell-pull across the room.

When the footman came in response to her summons she told him breathlessly, "Bring round my carriage and instruct my maid to fetch my bonnet and pelisse."

As the lackey withdrew Eliza put one hand to her aching head and valiantly fought back her tears which threatened to overcome her all the while. She had achieved a victory of sorts over Marisa Tarrazi, but even if that battle was won the war certainly was not over. Marisa Tarrazi would not give up her fight and she had the marquis firmly on her side. Eliza felt totally alone and quite helpless against the prevailing tide.

At the sight of his *chère amie* leaving the house, the marquis at first could not believe the evidence of his own eyes. He blinked and immediately saw he was not imagining her after all. He jumped down from the phaeton the moment it came to a halt, and handing the reins to his tiger he strode up to her, his face suffused with colour.

"Marisa, what in the name of the Devil are you doing here?"

His eyes were very dark and he seemed angry. However, Signora Tarrazi smiled and none of her own anger at the unsatisfactory interview was evident in her manner.

"I have been calling on Lady Emberay. A visit was long overdue."

His brow creased into a frown. "Not in my opinion." He

139

looked at her keenly. "You are not given to making social calls."

"How right you are. I would not normally be received by the top-lofty ladies of the *ton*, but I deemed it time to act and Lady Emberay had the good sense to receive me."

His anger had not abated one bit. "For what purpose?" he asked in a soft tone which none the less would have chilled anyone other than Marisa Tarrazi.

"If you do not like the sight of me here in your house, you may blame yourself. You have been exceeding tardy, *caro*. Now you will find Lady Emberay prepared for your request for a divorce."

She began to get into the carriage, but he caught hold of her arm and drew her back towards him. "You cannot—I cannot believe you have actually spoken of it to her. This is a jest, is it not, Marisa?"

The woman's eyes opened wide. "It certainly is not. Be sure that I did speak of it."

Fury seemed to fill his entire being. "How dare you! Do you know what you have done?"

He raised the driving-whip he still held in his hand, and Marisa Tarrazi's eyes widened with fear as she recoiled from his wrath. It was a side of him she had not witnessed before.

"No!" she cried. "I beg of you do not."

Then his arm dropped and she was able to draw a sigh of relief. "*Caro*, it was for our future."

He relinquished his hold on her arm to toss it away from him in disgust. "We have no future. Are you so stupid you cannot see that?"

"Do not say so! You are angry and I am sorry, but don't say things you cannot possibly mean."

"I have never meant anything more. My God, why did I not see you for the scheming baggage you are?"

"*Caro!*" she cried, shaking her head in bewilderment. "I beg of you don't be so cruel."

"What you have done this day is cruel." His lip curled

140

into a derisory sneer. "Did you really think I would abandon Eliza for you? Allow you to bring up my children? Be mistress of my house? Mrs. Tate, you have taken leave of your senses."

She gasped at the use of her real name, and then he turned on his heel and strode towards the house. "Max!" she cried, hurling herself after him, trying to catch hold of his coat. "Please don't leave me."

He didn't stop, but said, "I have said all I am going to say to you."

"Oh, I beg of you do not cast me off this way. Think of our love. Let me explain—I shall beg Lady Emberay's pardon, I vow to you. It was an error. I see it now. Just let me make amends and everything will be as it was. You know you will forgive me."

He paused by the door where the footmen were observing the scene with great enjoyment as were the coachmen in the courtyard. The marquis surveyed her dispassionately for the first time. "Yes, you poor, wretched creature, I can forgive you even though I cannot hope to forgive myself."

She drew back, clapping one hand to her lips, at last realising he had meant every word he had spoken to her. Her eyes brimmed as yet unshed tears.

"What am I to do?" she gasped.

"You still have your voice, Marisa, so be glad of that. If you have one iota of sense, my dear, you will pack your bandboxes and be out of London by the morrow."

The great oak door slammed shut behind him, and for a moment the singer stood transfixed on the step. Then she turned on her heel and hurled herself into her carriage. It left the courtyard just as Lady Emberay's barouche was driven in.

Eliza tied her bonnet-strings as she ran down the stairs. It was a struggle for Dorcas to keep up with her. However, Eliza hesitated halfway down the stairs when she saw her husband rush into the hall. The sight of him made her heart ache anew, for despite everything she still loved him as much as ever. He appeared to be uncharacteristically agitated, and it was some small measure of comfort for her to realise he had not known of Signora Tarrazi's visit until just now.

"Eliza!" he greeted her when he caught sight of her coming down the stairs. "Eliza, I must talk with you on a matter of the greatest urgency."

She ran down the last few steps and past him, avoiding looking directly at him, for if she did she knew her resolve would fail. He would charm her with a few soothing words, calm her fears with meaningless platitudes. Just then she wanted to remain angry, especially as he did not like it.

"I am afraid that is impossible, Max. I have an engagement for which I am already late. I have been detained too long already."

"A few moments of your time is all I ask."

She pulled on her gloves. "I have wasted enough time already. You will have to excuse me."

He drew in a deep breath and straightened up to full height. "Eliza, I insist that you stay."

She did pause to look at him then, coldly, and dispassionately, and then she hurried out of the house. He pursued her, but she climbed into the barouche all the same, sinking back into the squabs. To her relief he remained on the kerb and did not climb in after her.

"Very well, Elizabeth, by all means be angry," he said in an agitated way. "I own you are entitled to be angry with me."

She looked at him again. "You never call me Elizabeth unless *you* are angry, Max, but be assured I am not angry with you. I am merely late for my appointment. It is shockingly bad manners."

"You are angry. I know when you're angry, and I cannot blame it in you, only let me explain."

She smiled mirthlessly. "Do not trouble. Recall I am accustomed to your outrageous behaviour. I only hope that

Signora Tarrazi is prepared to deal with it in the future. Drive on, Scatchard.''

''No don't,'' the marquis countermanded, banging his hand on the side of the carriage.

''Drive on,'' Eliza repeated, and the poor fellow didn't know what to do.

''Are you meeting Lieutenant Peterson?'' the marquis demanded.

''Do drive on, Scatchard,'' Eliza repeated yet again, this time drawing the curtain across the window.

The carriage jerked forward, and she heard the marquis call her name followed by ''Hell and damnation!''

When she glanced out of the back window she saw him throw his driving-whip into the gutter before turning on his heel and striding into the house.

Eliza covered her face with her hands, giving in at last to her despair while her maid watched helplessly.

''Where to, my lady?'' the coachman asked.

She hadn't given a thought to that in her haste to escape a confrontation with her husband. ''Drive me to Knightsbridge,'' she answered after a moment. 'No, I wish to go further than that. Kensington. No, Scatchard, drive me to Richmond Park. It's further still.''

''Yes, my lady,'' he replied, and the carriage moved along more quickly and soon Piccadilly was far in the distance.

Eliza knew, though, however far she went, before long she would be obliged to return and face the moment she had been dreading for weeks.

FIFTEEN

"There have been a number of cards and messages left in your absence," the house-steward informed Eliza when she returned to the house, feeling as dispirited as when she had left. "The flowers are from Lieutenant Peterson and the marchpane from Sir Hugo Nuncton."

"Is his lordship at home?" she asked in a dull voice, glancing at the large bouquet of spring flowers. The sight of them gave her no pleasure, no more than the box of marchpane sent by Sir Hugo.

"No, my lady. He went out not long after you had left and he has not returned." Eliza had ignored all the messages, although in normal circumstances she would gather them up eagerly to read in her drawing-room. As she turned away the house-steward said, holding out the silver tray. "This note was delivered only a short while ago, my lady. The messenger said it was urgent and you were to have it as soon as you returned."

Eliza took it off the salver, recognising Lady Bramwell's hand and seal. With shaking hands she broke the seal and began to read.

"My dear Eliza. I beg of you to tell me what is afoot. If anything of interest is about to occur I demand to be the first to know." Eliza's lips quirked into a smile despite her inner misery. "Emberay has been calling upon every acquaintance you have ever had, searching for you, it seems. He has made no bones about it, which is quite unlike your husband. He even called at Denzil's lodgings. Imagine! Trusting to hear from you very soon. Rosamund Bramwell.''

As Eliza refolded the note and slipped it into her pocket she reflected sadly that he must be in a great hurry to marry that baggage. No doubt some other buck is pursuing her relentlessly too and he would not wish to lose her to another.

The house-steward was looking at her curiously. After a moment's hesitation she told him, ''When Lord Emberay returns, pray inform him I am indisposed and do not wish to be disturbed.''

''Yes, my lady,'' the servant replied, his face impassive.

His apparent disinterest in what was happening in the house was deceptive, she knew. The servants' hall would still be buzzing with speculation about the scene they had witnessed earlier. Although such altercations were commonplace in some houses of *beau monde*, the servants at Emberay House had never witnessed one of such magnitude between their master and mistress before.

Wondering how long she could delay the inevitable confrontation between them, Eliza walked slowly up the stairs and was about to go to her rooms and lie down when Anna came hurrying up to her.

''Thank the Lord you're back, my lady. I haven't known what to do.''

Immediately Eliza was jerked out of her dark thoughts by the anguished look on the girl's face. ''What is amiss, Anna?''

''It's Lord Aldan, my lady. He's awful ill.''

Eliza's eyes opened wide with fear. ''Ill? What in heaven's name do you mean by that?''

''The headache just got worse and worse, my lady, and now he's got a fever. I did all you said, but he kept getting worse. I just don't know what to do now.''

Eliza tossed her bonnet and pelisse onto a sofa in the

corridor and began to hurry towards the nursery, her heart full of dread. "Have one of the footmen go for a physician—Sir Franklyn Desmaine in Tavistock Square—and do tell him to hurry!"

Sir Franklyn Desmaine carefully made his examination of the child with meticulous care. All Eliza could think of as she twisted her damp handkerchief between her fingers was how young Kit looked in his large four-poster bed. He seemed to be no more than a baby.

At last the physician closed his bag, and it was a fearful Eliza who followed him from the room. In the corridor she immediately turned to face him. "Sir Franklyn, I beg of you to be honest with me; is it a serious matter?"

"Lord Aldan, I am afraid to tell you, is very ill indeed, my lady."

Eliza gasped. "Oh no, it cannot be."

"However," the physician added, smiling slightly, "he is strong and I do not entirely despair for his life."

"Then there is actually danger?" she asked, almost in a whisper.

"I regret to say so, my lady. It would not be just for me to pretend otherwise, but all is not hopeless, I assure you. It will be some time before the crisis is reached, and I shall, of course, call in at frequent intervals to check on his progress."

"Is there nothing else we can do?"

"I do suggest that the other child be kept away from the nursery."

"Lucy has already been sent to my sister-in-law in the country."

"Very wise."

"But there *must* be something else we can do, Sir Franklyn."

The physician smiled faintly. "I regret not, my lady. All that can be done with a fever of this kind is to keep the patient as comfortable as possible, and hope for a recovery."

"Hope is not a very potent medicine," Eliza cried, unable to keep the bitterness out of her voice.

"It is far more potent than you would believe." He bowed low before her. "My lady."

She watched him go and then laid her hand against the wainscot as tears streamed down her cheeks. After a few minutes she straightened up again, wiped her cheeks and blew her nose, realising that such weakness could help no one, and she knew she would have to be strong. She had just steeled herself to go back into the nursery when the marquis came hurrying around the corner.

"Eliza! My God, what has happened?"

She froze, unable to look at him, for she knew her despair and bitterness could so easily spill forth at that moment. His eyes were as bleak as hers as he stared down at her. "I have just spoken with Sir Franklyn Desmaine. I cannot believe Kit can be so ill."

"Be certain that he is," she answered dully. "He doesn't even know me."

She put her hand on the door-knob, and he said, "Eliza, let me—"

"I can think of nothing but Kit just now. I beg you leave me alone to nurse him."

He followed her into the room where Anna was hovering by the bed. "There is no point in your being here, Eliza," he told her. "Anna is quite capable of taking care of him."

"I have every intention of remaining here at his side," Eliza answered in a voice devoid of all expression. "Be certain I shall not leave his side until—until he is recovered."

The marquis drew a sigh of resignation and then brought up a chair for her. "Very well. If that is what you wish." She sat down, scarcely taking her eyes off the child who

147

was not aware of her presence. The marquis stepped back. "If there is any change let me know. I shall remain here in the house until there is some news."

Eliza glanced up at him, an angry retort about Marisa Tarrazi awaiting him hovering on her lips, but then she bit it back, knowing, whatever his faults and weaknesses, he was fond of his children. Instead she nodded, and a moment later the door clicked shut behind him.

The physician returned some time later, but he could give Eliza no more comfort than before, except to say, "In my opinion the crisis is near and, therefore, I shall return before long, my lady."

The marquis returned some time later to find Eliza resting her weary head on her hand which was propped on the edge of the bed. He came quietly across the room, saying in a half whisper, "Is there any news?"

"None," she answered wearily.

"He—is not—worse, is he?"

"He is burning up," Eliza replied in a broken voice. "It is hopeless and I can do nothing."

The marquis put his hand on her shoulder. "Eliza, you must rest. It cannot help Kit if you are ill too. You can do nothing here except torture yourself. Come away and rest a while."

"I cannot rest until—I know."

He put his arms around her and raised her from the chair. She looked round without really seeing him. "*I* shall stay here while you rest, Eliza."

"No—" she protested, but he led her to a sofa at the far side of the room and made her sit down on it. "I shan't leave his side, you may be certain."

Her head swam and she seemed to have no strength to resist any longer. He lifted her legs onto the sofa and a moment later brought her a pillow and a blanket. When he had put the blanket over her he stood at the side of the sofa looking down at her as tears slid silently down her cheeks.

"Eliza—"

She looked up at him. "Vow to me you will call me if there is any change at all."

He smiled faintly. "You may rely upon it."

It seemed to be only a short time later when she heard him calling her name in an urgent tone. Immediately Eliza got to her feet and ran across to the bed where the marquis was standing with a tearful Anna at his side. He glanced anxiously towards Eliza.

"What is it?" she asked fearfully.

"I think he may be a little better, but I cannot be certain. Tell me what you think."

Eliza leaned over her son and smoothed back a damp lock of hair from his brow. As she did so his eyelids fluttered and then he looked directly up at her. "Mama."

"Yes, dearest, I am here. How do you feel? A little better?"

"My headache has gone and I feel terribly hungry. I think I've missed my dinner."

Eliza smiled through a mist of tears. "More than one dinner, my love. You shall have some gruel as soon as Sir Franklyn says you may."

"Do I have to wait?"

"Well, perhaps not," his mother replied, sounding doubtful.

"I do hate gruel." He looked at the marquis then. "Papa, what are you doing here?"

"I'm here to make absolutely certain you receive some nourishment before long."

The child smiled faintly. "I'm glad. It doesn't matter what anyone else says, it's you who issues the orders in this house."

"And you may be certain I shall instruct Cook to make whatever food you want."

Whether he heard the promise or not none of them really knew, for he had fallen asleep, peacefully and naturally. Eliza straightened up at last, clenching both hands into fists.

"Thank God." She felt her husband's hand on her shoulder, and when she looked at him she thought that this was something Marisa Tarrazi could never share with him. She wondered if he might be thinking something similar too, for there was an odd expression on his face.

He was very close to her, and suddenly aware of it she began to tremble uncontrollably. Again he looked anxious, but on this occasion his concern was for her.

"Eliza?"

She took a step backwards, wanting only to put some distance between them, but he moved quickly too. He looked so odd, suddenly, and his voice seemed to be such a long way away, although she knew full well that it wasn't so.

Eliza heard him say, "Anna, send one of the footmen to discover if Sir Franklyn is on his way."

Eliza's head swam. A moment later she felt his arms go about her which made her begin to tremble again. When she put one hand up to his face his cheeks felt rough.

"How long—has Kit been ill?"

"Two days. You must sit down, Eliza—"

"Signora Tarrazi will wonder where you—"

The sentence was never finished. Eliza felt his arms tighten about her and heard him calling her name, but she felt only a blessed oblivion at last.

The book was one of the latest novels, delivered to the house by a concerned acquaintance, but Eliza could not become interested in it. She put it down and got up from the day-bed to walk restlessly across to the window. The garden was beginning to burgeon with spring flowers, dormant bushes were slowly returning to life. At that part of the house she might well have been miles from the hurry-scurry of Piccadilly which was in reality very close by.

As she glanced out at the neat lawns and well-ordered flower-beds she couldn't help but recall her arrival there as a new bride. How frightened she had been of the new responsibility thrust upon her at such an early age. She remembered doubting her ability to put the house to rights, to supervise the entertaining expected of the Marchioness of Emberay. There were a few of her contemporaries who expected her to fail, no doubt at the same time hoping she would do so, for Eliza had been fully aware there were many who envied her such a dashing and handsome husband as well as an elevated position in the *beau monde*.

But she had not failed. Although her husband had never actually said so, she had always been of the opinion he was satisfied with their life together. Most certainly he had been delighted with her after the birth of their son. Now Marisa Tarrazi had changed all that. He was no longer satisfied with his wife or their mode of life together. Whatever effort she had put into the marriage, which could so easily have been a disaster from the first, was all for nothing after all.

Eliza sighed deeply as she came away from the window at last. Rosamund Bramwell would bear witness to the fact she had put up a fight, but it was well and truly lost and she was resigned to the ending of her marriage.

A soft knock at the door made her start out of her melancholy thoughts. After a moment or two she gave the summons to enter, fully expecting to see a servant bearing yet another pile of cards and bouquets of flowers. The room was already full of their pungent scent. There was even a large basket of flowers from the marquis. She wasn't surprised by his gesture, although she was aware it meant nothing.

It was not, however, a servant who entered the room. Eliza was taken aback to see her husband standing in the

151

doorway, looking as debonair as ever in his outdoor clothes.

As he glanced across the room at her he looked slightly surprised. "So, you're up, Eliza. That really is excellent. I'm very pleased to see you recovered, and so much sooner than anyone expected."

She smiled, feeling as awkward as she had when she first met him. Conversation then had been difficult for both of them too. "I am fully recovered, I thank you."

"That is a great relief to me. I feared you too had a fever."

"Oh no, Sir Franklyn tells me it was merely exhaustion, and I am well rested now." She laced her fingers together and took a deep breath. "Tell me, how is Kit today?"

The marquis came further into the room, and his rather strained expression softened somewhat. "Fretting to be allowed out to play, so we may assume he is well on the way to recovery."

Eliza smiled quite genuinely. "That is such a relief." Then her smile faded. "Some days ago, after Signora Tarrazi's visit, you said you wished to talk with me. As we are both aware, circumstances prevented it at that time, but I am of the opinion we should come to some amicable arrangement with no further delay."

He walked quickly towards her. "How can I begin to beg your pardon for causing you so much pain?"

She laughed harshly. "That is of no account now. What is of more import is to deal with each other in a civilised manner. We have always done so in the past."

"One thing I must say to you, Eliza; your happiness is paramount to me."

She smiled, unable to hide her bitterness. "How considerate of you, Max."

He was looking at her and was unusually ill at ease. "Tell me what you wish to do, Eliza."

Her mouth was suddenly dry. She couldn't look at him.

"Surely it is what you wish to do which is more to the point."

"All I wish to do is elicit some measure of forgiveness from you, although I am fully aware I don't deserve any such consideration. I have behaved so badly."

Eliza walked towards the window once again. "I'm fully aware it isn't always possible to be in control of one's behaviour when one is in love, and I have known for some considerable time how much you loved Signora Tarrazi. I did not need to wait until she came here to tell me so."

"I was certainly infatuated with her," he protested, "but I was not and could never be in love with her." His voice softened. "I love only you, Eliza."

She turned to face him again, her heart missing a beat. He was looking at her hopefully. "Is it too late? Has Lieutenant Peterson taken my place in your heart?"

"No," she answered breathlessly. "No one can ever do that, and Lieutenant Peterson has always been fully aware of it."

He went to take her trembling hands in his. "I have been suffering some kind of lunacy which I vow to you is over now. It will never happen again."

"Does Signora Tarrazi know?"

He smiled faintly. "I have made my feelings known to her and I'm given to understand she has left London for an indefinite engagement in Dublin." Eliza closed her eyes and offered a silent prayer of thankfulness. "It seems," he was saying, "as if I have been seeking something for a long time without knowing what I really sought was here all the time."

She raised her eyes slowly to meet his. "I have waited so long to hear you say so."

"If you'll condescend to forgive my foolishness I shall spend the rest of my days telling you I love you. You'll never have cause to doubt it again."

Her eyes glowed with love and thankfulness. "I love

you too, so there is really no need to speak of forgiveness. Your love is all I wanted and I can be content now.''

He kissed her gently at first and then with a hunger to which she responded whole-heartedly. At last she drew away, saying breathlessly, ''You have never kissed me like that before.''

Not relinquishing his hold on her he replied, whispering in her ear, ''Then it is long past the time I should have begun.''

She relaxed against him, saying in a wistful tone, ''When Kit was so ill I thought, if he was spared, I could bear anything, but I realise now I couldn't survive losing you.''

''If it is any consolation to you, my love, you were in very little danger of doing so. I was more in fear of losing you.''

He kissed her again before drawing away. She watched perplexedly as he went quickly to the door and turned the key in the lock. ''What *are* you doing?'' she asked, laughing in bewilderment.

''Just in the event we are disturbed.''

She laughed again as he came back across the room. The weeks of misery and uncertainty seemed to be a long way away now. ''Who is like to do so at this time of the day?''

He smiled wryly. ''The servants, although they can be sent away quite easily.'' Unexpectedly, he frowned. ''It is not always so easy with my sister.''

''Horatia?'' Eliza looked astonished as he pulled her down onto the day-bed and drew her into his arms again. ''Horatia is back?''

''I regret to say that is so.''

''I have no notion she planned to return just yet, but then,'' she added wryly, ''of late I have been very much preoccupied with my own problems.''

He sighed. ''When Horatia had word that Lucy was on

her way to Wychcombe and the reason for it, she started out for London immediately. It's possible she doubts our ability to deal with a crisis in her absence. In any event, I have already been obliged to endure at least ten minutes of her scolding."

"For what possible reason?" Eliza asked, still amused.

"Needless to say, everything which has happened is because of my failings."

"How unjust," Eliza protested. "Kit's illness was none of your doing."

"*Everything* untoward which happens in this household is my doing, in Horatia's opinion." He suddenly looked wry. "I can only be glad she does not know the worst of it."

"Poor Max," Eliza crooned.

"On this occasion I cannot complain, for I deserved the set-down," he conceded. "In view of all that has happened, I am fortunate to have escaped retribution so lightly." He considered her for a long moment before asking softly, "Did you care deeply for Lieutenant Peterson?"

For a brief moment Eliza was tempted to confess that their relationship was mainly contrived, but then she said impishly, "He amused me at a time when I badly needed diverting, and therefore I am greatly indebted to him and always will be."

His eyes grew dark. "If I'd lost you, Eliza, it would have been my own fault for driving you into his arms."

"I'm here in your arms now," she reminded him.

He kissed her again, and after a few moments neither of them cared if the entire *beau monde* came knocking on the door. It remained firmly locked.

More romance from Regency and...

RACHELLE EDWARDS

Available at your bookstore or use this coupon.

____DANGEROUS DANDY	20906	2.50
____THE SCOUNDREL'S DAUGHTER	20843	2.25
____FORTUNE'S CHILD	50222	1.50
____THE MARRIAGE BARGAIN	50288	1.50
____THE RANSOM INHERITANCE	21126	2.50

FAWCETT MAIL SALES
Dept. TAF, 201 E. 50th St., New York, N.Y. 10022

Please send me the FAWCETT BOOKS I have checked above. I am en-
closing $....................(add 50¢ per copy to cover postage and handling).
Send check or money order—no cash or C.O.D.'s please. Prices and
numbers are subject to change without notice. Valid in U.S. only. All orders
are subject to availability of books.

Name_____

Address_____

City_____State_____Zip Code_____

14   Allow at least 4 weeks for delivery.   TAF-65